Six Ways from Sunday

By **Mercy Celeste**

Stephanie,
All my Best
Mercy Celeste

Copyright

Six Ways from Sunday is a work of fiction. Names, characters, places, and incidents are the product of the author's imagination or are used fictitiously. Any resemblance to actual persons, living or dead, events, or locales is entirely coincidental.

Copyright © 2013 by Mercy Celeste

ISBN-13: 978-1484889077
ISBN-10: 148488907X

Edited by Jason Huffman

All rights reserved.

Published in the United States by Mercy Celeste

Warning: All rights reserved. No part of this book may be reproduced in any many without written permission, except for brief quotations embodied in critical articles and reviews.

The unauthorized reproduction or distribution of this copyrighted work is illegal. Criminal copyright infringement, including infringement without monetary gain is investigated by the FBI and is punishable by up to five years in federal prison and a fine of $250,000.

eBooks are not transferable. They cannot be sold, shared or given away, as it is an infringement on the copyright of this book.

Contact the publisher for further information:

celeste.mercy@yahoo.com

Cover Art provided by Reece Notley

Acknowledgement: I would like to thank Kendall McKenna for the time she took away from her own writing to help me craft Dylan's Marine Corps background. I couldn't have managed any of that on my own and am extremely grateful for her patience and incredible knowledge of all things Marine

Trade Mark Acknowledgements:
Skype
Jack Daniels
Disney

Dedication

I'm dedicating this book to a school. On December 25, 2012 Murphy High School in Mobile, Alabama was hit by a tornado. The school is an historic landmark in the state with beautiful tiled roofs stucco walls. It is also the high school my three oldest children attended. My third daughter is currently a student at Murphy and this past semester has been trying. All students were relocated to portables at a middle school so that the school could continue without splitting the students up. Repairs and renovations are currently underway but the damage was extensive, all of the buildings are uninhabitable. I dedicate this book to the school and to the students, past and present who lost a part of them on Christmas day.

If you would like to donate to the tornado relief fund please contact the Murphy Alumni Association at this link http://www.murphyalumni.org/

Thanks so much,
Mercy

Chapter One

"When were you going to tell me?" The slamming door brought Dylan up short as Hurricane Bowen swept into the room bringing chaos in his wake. "I had to find out from the mail lady. The mail lady, Dylan!"

Dylan glanced around at the baskets of laundry, packing boxes, and luggage then winced. "Bo." He had no idea what to say. Or how to explain. "I was going to tell you tonight."

"Are you sure you weren't going to wait until I was gone and just run off and..." Bo raked his hand through his short hair, making it stand up on end. He wore swim trunks that were at the moment dripping onto the carpet. His golden body shimmered from the pool. His gaze roamed the room, taking in the disorder that occupied the usually tidy space. "You enlisted? In the Marines? Come on Dyl, tell me she was lying. Tell me you aren't...fuck you *are* leaving me, aren't you?" he shouted when his gaze came to rest on the piece of luggage in front of Dylan.

Dylan could feel the rage coursing through his friend from across the room. And that made him angry. "*I'm* leaving you? Pardon me, but who is the one having the going away party tonight?"

Bo stopped staring at the open suitcase. Dylan was trying to whittle his worldly possessions down to one small bag but so much of it couldn't be left behind. He'd agonized all morning, sorting things to go into storage or to get rid of completely. One small bag of things he'd need and the things he couldn't live without. The picture of the two of them taken right after the State win in December, both in uniform and sweaty, was on top. He couldn't leave that behind.

"I'm just going to school, only a couple hundred miles from here. You're going to...they'll send you to war. You can't go." Bo took the frame from its place on top of the few items of clothing Dylan had packed and held it like a shield. "I won't let you."

"You won't let me?" Dylan stopped folding the t-shirt in his hands, or twisting it, he'd stopped folding long before. "I wasn't scouted and I didn't get a scholarship. Big Man Bowen Murphy is going all the way to the NFL and I'm not going to stay home pining for him."

"You could have come with me. You could have gone to school and maybe gotten a walk-on tryout." Hope entered his friend's eyes, a hope that Dylan didn't want to kill. But he had no choice.

"I can't go to school, Bo, not this year. There's no money. I don't qualify for financial aid because on paper there is money. But there isn't. Dad left tons of debt. Mom is going to sell the house. The insurance barely covered his funeral. Maybe next year. But next year—"

"Next year you'll be in Iraq or Afghanistan. The year after, probably Iran or Syria. Or hell, maybe we'll invade Mars in the next year. Or you'll be dead." Fear tinged his voice. One thing about Bowen was his no fear mentality. Take no prisoners. Show no fear. Beat them at their own game in their own house. That's why he had the big scholarship and the bright future. All the way back to pee wee league it had been the same. Bo, the big chunky boy who didn't talk much, but no one pushed him down. No one pushed Dylan down either. They'd have Bo to deal with. Bo and Dylan. Dylan and Bo. They were a team. A unit. Where one went, the other wasn't far behind.

Except now, Dylan had to stand on his own. "I can't be dead. You'd fly over and take on the whole Middle East if that happened." He tried to laugh it off. Hoping to make Bo accept that this wasn't such a bad thing.

"Why didn't you tell me?" So much for that idea. Bo threw the frame against the wall, the force of impact shattered the wood and glass, and the photo fell face down in the pile of debris.

"You asshole, why'd you do that?" Dylan was across the room before he knew what he was doing. He shoved Bo as hard as he could, but that was like shoving a brick wall. A brick wall that shoved back and Dylan landed on the floor. Bo followed him down, straddling him; his fist raised just enough to punch. He was so close Dylan could see the fear and anger in his eyes. Betrayal. This was betrayal, something he'd never seen before. Something he'd never done before. Dylan steeled himself for the blow but it didn't come.

A drop of moisture on his nose made him open his eyes in time to see Bo swipe at his eyes. "You can undo it? Please, undo it. Go tell them you made a mistake. Tell them that you can't go." He lowered his hand and leaned over, his face so close Dylan could see every pore, every single blond growth of stubble. He could see Bo's fear...and smell it. See and smell and feel, enough to react when he'd sworn he wouldn't. This was something he had to do and there was nothing left to decide.

"I can't," Dylan whispered, swallowing back the thick greasy bile that threatened to climb out his throat. He couldn't allow Bo's fear to engulf him. He'd never be able to leave if he did.

"Why? You always wanted football. There are other colleges. There are ways—"

"I want to go," Dylan said, ignoring the pain in his friend's voice. He'd never told Bo that football wasn't his dream. Bo's dream had always been big enough for them both. Until it wasn't anymore. Senior year was spectacular but he'd known early on that he wasn't anything special. He was just an average run of the mill quarterback and the recruiters had too many quarterbacks with so-so arms.

They came to see Bo play, Badass Bowen Murphy who could snatch a fly out of thin air and take on the biggest meanest lineman any team could throw at him, that's what the recruiters wanted. He was big and agile and poetry in motion. "Football is your dream, Bowen. My talents lie elsewhere."

"You always did like to talk about the future but this isn't what we talked about. I can't see you with a gun in your hand." His voice took on a wheedling childlike tone. One he used when they were six or seven and in trouble. All the time in trouble.

"Not all military jobs end up on the battlefield." But Dylan knew that Bo knew he lied. If he'd wanted a safe computer job, he would have joined a different branch of the military. He was born to be a Marine like his father, and his grandfather before him. He was born to serve the way they had.

"Promise me you won't get dead." Tears clogged Bo's throat, he made an impatient noise and leaned over until his nose touched Dylan's. "Promise me you'll write. Email. Whatever they let you do, every day. And that you don't get dead."

"I promise." Trapped by his friend's hazel gaze, Dylan gulped down the lump in his throat, but it wouldn't go away. He'd write every day. He'd Skype.

Everything he could. He couldn't promise that other thing. But he didn't need to tell Bo that. "I promise. You won't even notice I'm gone."

Bo nodded, his jaw clenched and unclenched, he breathed out a quick breath. One that smelled of orange soda. And then Dylan tasted the orange soda, on his lips, his tongue. Shocked, he didn't realize why his mouth was fused to Bo's until Bo sat up. His dick hard and straining beneath the wet trunks. The look in his eyes wild, embarrassed—no, ashamed. Shame and fear. So much fear that turned to confusion.

Confusion echoing in his own mind, Dylan caught his arm before Bo could clamber off him. Holding on for all he was worth, he said the words he thought he never could. "Kiss me! Again! Please."

* * * * *

The buzzing of humiliation and shame was all Bo could hear. The look on Dylan's face, shock, fear, loathing…not loathing. Why was Dylan looking at him as if he'd lost his damned mind? Because he had. Time to go. Play it off as… as what? Stupidity? The buzzing in his mind intensified the longer Dylan stared at him. His lips moved but Bo didn't hear a word his friend said, his fingers dug into Bo's arms, effectively keeping him from running. He hadn't meant to kiss Dylan, he didn't actually know that he had, except that Dylan's tongue was in his mouth and then he knew what he'd done.

Held captive by the death grip on his arms and the stunned look in Dyl's eyes, he straddled his best friend, his dick so damned hard he'd come if Dylan so much as looked at it. Dylan's shorts and t-shirt were wet where he'd dripped onto him. A thick bulge beneath the loose cotton shorts caught his attention but he wouldn't let himself think about that right now. No way did Dylan have a hard-on for him. No way. He couldn't breathe or think or run. All these years of keeping this shit from Dylan. Of wanting to be with him. Football and Dylan. That was all he'd ever wanted. Now he had football but was losing Dylan. But Dylan seemed to be saying what he wanted to hear. He wanted so much to do as Dylan asked, but then he'd confirm what Dylan already suspected. No way was he willing to risk that much no matter how many times Dyl licked his lips and said the word. Yet he couldn't stop staring at the word on those lips.

Bo didn't lean over and do what the lips asked for. He remained frozen, hovering above his friend, blood pumping too fast in some places and too slowly in others. His brain for example, no blood at all in there. He had no idea how the thing even worked anymore.

Dylan did a half crunch, holding Bo's arms to keep himself in the position, and kissed him. God, it was like, god, and god…Dyl's lips were so damned soft, his tongue hot, wet, insistent. Bo opened his mouth and inhaled like a man rescued from drowning. Breathing through his nose, he crushed Dylan to his chest. And then they were flat on the floor again, body to body, mouth to mouth, dick to dick.

"Why didn't you ever tell me?" The words were an imitation of his from earlier, but different. Softer, full of wonder and regret. Bo had no answer besides the obvious.

"Why didn't you?" He forgot what the question was or why he wasn't supposed to be on the floor humping his best friend. Dylan's hands slid along his back, lover-like. Exploring him, delving inside his swim trunks. Fingernails dug into his ass cheeks. He moaned into Dylan's open mouth. His hips took on a mind of their own, rocking his excruciatingly hard cock along the hard ridge trapped beneath him. His skin dried only to become sweat soaked as he moved.

"Take these off." Dylan pushed at his trunks, shoving them down around his thighs. Bo did as he was told and shimmied the wet material down and off. When he was finished, he grasped the waistband of Dylan's shorts and yanked, tearing the thin fabric in his haste to find the heat he craved. "My shirt." Dylan grunted against his mouth. In a couple of seconds, they were naked, together, very together on the carpet in Dylan's living room.

"Where's your mom?" Seemed an important question now that there could be no explaining away what they did.

Dylan slid his mouth along Bo's neck, licking him as he went. "Work, she's on her long shift. You taste so fucking good. I knew you would." The wonder of discovery in his words had Bo shaking. This couldn't be real. This wasn't happening. Dylan's breath caught, he trembled, his mouth still doing wicked things to Bo's neck. He couldn't stop the need to grind himself into his friend. God help him.

Bo moved his knees in between Dylan's legs and lowered himself to the floor. Dylan didn't complain about being trapped beneath him. He made a sound in his throat, one that made Bo's blood boil. Helpless, hopeless, mindless pleasure, oh god, yes. Dylan moved with him, rubbing his dick to Bo's, small gasps as shocks of electricity raced between them. Bo could feel him shiver. Dylan's eyes were hooded and dark. He'd never seen him look this way before. As if he…oh, god, this was good. Like nothing he'd ever expected or could have hoped for. That Dylan wanted the same thing…god, this was sex and this was Dylan and it was so damned easy. They could have had this all along or maybe Dyl had and he hadn't and—

"Who?" He didn't know how to ask. The question was too important. Girls were always around. They both dated. But Dylan never bragged about anyone not even to him. Had he been with another guy? Would Dyl have told him if he had?

"No one. Only wanted you." The words tumbled out of Dylan's kiss swollen mouth as he wrapped his long lean legs around Bo's hips. "Too afraid to—I didn't know how to—or if you would—"

Relief flooded him. Dylan and him, together. He wanted this, he'd dreamed of this. "Yeah, me too, no one. Dreamed of doing this, with you. So much…this feels so good, better than I imagined." He found Dylan's lips again and sucked his tongue into his mouth. The need to do more than just rub against his friend sizzled in his mind. He gripped Dylan's hips and thrust hard against him as he tried to get closer. Hot slippery pre-come coated them, making it easy to move. Dylan gasped, arching his hips off the floor at the same time Bo thrust upward. And they both froze.

A cry of pain from Dylan confirmed what he felt. Somehow he'd managed to slip inside his friend. Just past the crown of his dick. But deep enough to know that he never wanted to pull out, except this couldn't hurt Dylan. He wouldn't force it. "Don't." Dylan whispered, his voice gone rough, eyes flaring wide as Bo moved to withdraw. "It's okay. Just slowly, okay."

Bo stared into his friend's eyes, looking for the truth. "You want me to…" He couldn't bring himself to say the words. He didn't want to put a name to this. Not yet.

"Fuck me," Dylan finished for him, his face going scarlet, but his eyes burned bright and never left Bo's. He rocked his ass onto Bo's dick, wincing as he stretched. "We need lube. Don't...want to stop to...mmmm." Pain darkened his face, but only for a moment before his eyes turned...was that what they meant when they said lust? Whatever it was he saw in Dylan's eyes, he didn't want to lose it. "Just don't stop, okay."

Bo moved onto his knees, careful not to thrust deep inside as his body demanded. Dylan's arms flopped onto the floor. His skin flushed a deep red, his breath coming in fast gasps. Hard toned muscles everywhere Bo looked. But he knew what Dylan looked like. He'd seen him like this so many times. In the locker room, or the pool, hell, just changing after school. But never spread out on the floor with Bo's dick half inside him. Or with Dylan's dick lying long and hard against his belly, pre-come pooling around his navel. No, this was new.

"You're beautiful. Did you know?"

"I always thought the same about you." Dyl's smile was shy, hesitant, his blue eyes lit from inside with a fire Bo had never seen before. "It's okay, Bo, I want you to be the one."

The one to what? Take his virginity? Fuck him hard and send him off to Afghanistan with happy memories? Because Bo didn't want just one time. He wanted a lifetime. He'd known as much in tenth grade. But Dylan had never even looked at him. Not like he did now.

"Okay. Yeah, okay. Slow, right. Slow and it'll be fine. Okay." Bo did the only thing he could think of, he spit in his hand like he'd seen it done in the videos. He coated Dylan's hole and with more spit, his dick, hoping it would be enough. And then he pushed inside. Slowly, watching Dylan's eyes for his cue to stop or go deeper.

He went deeper. Dylan cried out, digging nail marks into Bo's arms. "Fuck," he said several times, "oh, fuck." But he didn't stop Bo, he moved with him with each miniscule thrust and withdraw, until Bo was inside him as far as he could go.

"God, don't move," Bo moaned, the tight heat surrounding him nearly unbearable. All of the blood in his body centered there. His head swam. The urge to come sizzled down his spine. He laid his head on Dylan's shoulder as he fought to catch his breath. "I'll come if you move."

Soft fingers stroked his face, he could feel Dylan's dick throbbing against his belly. "I'll come with you if I move. You feel so good inside me."

"Shit, Dylan, this can't be happening." But it was. He caught Dylan's lips as he moved over him, tongue thrusting into his friend's mouth, telling him what he wanted to do to him with his lower body if he dared to move. The throaty sounds Dylan made drove him to madness. He moved, hips rocking so damned slowly into Dylan's hot tight body, he thought he'd burn up from the friction.

"Fuck, fuck," Dylan cried against his mouth, his body going stiff, his hands slapped at Bo's back and then his ass. He gripped him there, holding him tight, straining to bring him inside deeper. "Fuuuuhhk!" Heat erupted between them, the musky scent inflaming Bo. He drove himself deep, short inelegant thrusts. Orgasm hit him fast and hard. Dylan held him as he emptied himself of years of longing and hours of fantasizing. Dylan's moan mingled with his. It was too much. All he could do was tremble like a little kid hiding from a monster. "Fuck," Dylan said one more time, his legs falling limp to the floor.

"Yeah, fuck," Bo agreed. Because now they were. Fucked. Fucked in every way possible. "I think I may have spooged on your mom's carpet."

Dylan laughed, his body shaking with the effort. "Somehow, I don't think she'll care."

"Are you okay, I mean, with this," Bo eased himself off his friend to withdraw. Dylan threw his head back and gasped as Bo pulled out. He looked so—what? Beautiful? Well fucked? Lying on the floor, his skin flushed and sweaty, his eyes glazed and languid, his arms limp, boneless. Yeah, the most beautiful thing he'd ever seen. Dylan was beautiful after fucking. Too damned beautiful.

"I'm good," Dylan said his voice ragged, raw. He rolled onto his side and Bo followed. He lay facing his friend, his head pillowed on his arm. "How about you? Regret setting in now that we've done the deed?"

Maybe. He didn't know. But he shook his head just the same. "No. No regret. When do you leave?" The shock that had driven him next door gone now, cold hard terror still held on. "For basic?"

"Boot camp and I leave next week. After I help Mom move into an apartment closer to the hospital. Most of this stuff is going into storage or she's going to sell it." Bo winced, he knew that since Dylan's dad had died they were having problems. He just didn't know it was this bad. "It's the mortgage, Bo, she can't manage it on her own. And really, with me gone what does she need this big house for?"

"I guess it's what's best. Doesn't mean I have to like the idea that you won't be right next door anymore." There was so much he wanted to say. He'd already made a fool of himself by demanding that Dylan unenlist.

Dylan didn't say anything for a moment then he sighed, and glanced away. "You won't be here anyway, it'll be the same as it would have been if I went to another college. We'd email, text, whatever, and that would be it."

He was right, of course he was right. And Bo was an idiot for thinking anything different. "But you would come home for the holidays."

"And you wouldn't be here because of post season games. Your summers will be short for training camps. You won't be here to miss me." Hope fled even before it could swell, Dylan was right. Dylan was always right and he hated that much about him.

"But I'll miss you. I already miss you and I haven't left yet." He swiped his thumb across Dylan's chin, the patch of stubble there rough under his touch.

"I know. I hate leaving you. I was looking for a way to tell you. I couldn't. I wasn't supposed to go until late fall but I was called up early. I thought there would be more time." Dylan hunted around for his shirt, finding his torn shorts, he sighed and wiped the rapidly drying cum from Bo's chest, and then his own. "It feels strange to have cum in my ass."

The shock of the words brought back the enormity of what they'd done. He'd just fucked his best friend. And wanted to do it again. "I should have pulled out like they do in the pornos and jacked off in your mouth. Would you have liked that better?"

The blush that crept up Dylan's chest into his face made Bo happy. "Watch much porn, do we?"

It was Bo's turn to blush. "Yeah, I had this problem with wanting to molest this hot guy who I thought was straight. Kept me sane. Watching gay porn, that is, not molesting hot guys… thinking I could have something like that."

"Yeah," Dylan whispered, his eyes going vacant for a moment as if Bo had hit a sore spot and then he smiled. "You really think I'm hot?"

"Since about sixth grade. Didn't dare tell you—football, you know. I wanted to keep it. And you were there so I thought, maybe that was all I needed."

"I wish you would have said something or done something sooner. We could have had more time." The smile in

Dylan's eyes lasted for about a second and then reality set in. Tomorrow this would be just a memory.

"We have tonight. I could sleep over," he suggested, hope flaring. Dylan's mom usually worked through the night and then slept for the next day or so. She wouldn't notice that anything other than their usual Friday-night-after-the-game-all-night-movie-fests-because-they-were-both-too-amped-up-to-sleep was going on in her house. They could have spent so many of those nights fucking. God, he wanted to taste Dylan's dick. Just once.

"What about your party? Everyone we went to school with will be at your house tonight."

Bo groaned, he was supposed to be cleaning the pool but the mail lady brought a package around and started chatting about the both of them leaving and how it wouldn't be the same with them both gone. In that moment he wanted nothing more than to call everyone and tell them to stay the fuck home. "I forgot. We can sneak off. Up to my room. Watch videos and—"

"Bo? Where the hell are you?" Bo groaned again, his father's voice carried through the open windows. "The pool isn't finished and your guests will be here in two hours."

"Oh fuck, I hope he didn't just hear us. I forgot I turned the air conditioner off and opened the windows." Dylan shoved his trunks at him and pushed him to his feet. His face going white for a moment. "After the party, sleep over here. They'll understand. Bring the videos. And anything else you have stashed away."

"I don't care if he did, he'll find out one day. Today would be good as any." Bo scrambled to pull his trunks on. Dylan stretched on the floor, a slight smile on his face. He never was shy about his body. Never. "I really want to suck your dick," Bo said before he could stop the thought from becoming words. The mentioned organ twitched and danced against Dylan's body.

"Tonight." Dylan ran his hand down his belly to cup his dick, his smile held so much promise. "I'm going to hold you to that."

"Bo! I'm not kidding, get your ass home now or I'm canceling this damn party," his father shouted, his voice closer now, most likely he was leaning over the fence.

"I'll be there in a minute," he yelled back, before dropping back to the floor. Unsure now, he touched his lips to Dylan's, the hand in his hair told him he was doing something right. "Maybe if I stay he'll follow through with the threat," he whispered, not wanting to leave now that he knew the truth. "I'd rather stay here."

Dylan shoved at his shoulder. "Give me a little while to finish up the laundry and I'll come over to help. Maybe we can do stuff in the pool, you know, when they're not looking."

"Yeah?" Bo's skin prickled with chills. What the hell could they do in the pool, in plain sight?

"Yeah, now go home before your dad comes looking for you and finds me lying here with a boner." And with those words, Bo was in the same condition. He'd have to jump in the pool to hide his erection.

"Okay," he said, biting his lip to stifle a groan. "Don't take too long. I need all the help I can get."

He left Dylan lying on the carpet and went back to his own yard, jumping straight in the deep end before his dad could say anything. When he came out the other side he had his body under control. As long as he didn't think about the night to come. Or how fast he could get this party to wind down. He had one night left with Dylan to tide him over for probably years. He pretended that the pool water was all that trickled down his face and got back to cleaning the filter before his dad came back out to clean the grill.

*****

The drive to the airport was silent. Most of the last week had been silent. Dylan stared out the window at the interstate traffic or trees passing by. At one point he could have sworn he saw a coyote standing on the side of the road. It was still very early and he'd had very little sleep; he was sure he was hallucinating because last time he checked there were no coyotes in Florida. The past night he'd Skyped with Bo until around three in the morning knowing that his plane left at nine and it was a long drive up to Tallahassee. Bo was miserable. Full out two-a-days in August was kicking his ass and he just didn't want to say goodbye.

"Dylan?" his mom said softly not quite an hour into the drive. She sounded wary, and tired, maybe a little angry but he couldn't tell. After what she'd seen last week and how she'd reacted, he was lucky she'd even offered to drive him to the airport.

"Yeah, Mom?" He really didn't want to talk about it. His feelings were too new. Too raw. The last night he and Bo had been together was the best night of his life. They'd done things that he'd only seen in porn. Bo's mouth on him had been incredible. He'd fallen asleep every night since, aching for more of that. But they'd overslept and Bo's mom had called to tell him they were ready to go and his mom had come to relay that message and walked in on them. And they'd been very naked, and very much sleeping together as in *sleeping together*. After she'd screamed and slammed the door, it had been icily quiet for days.

"Just tell me how long," she said softly, her eyes straight ahead, her knuckles white on the wheel as if she would strangle it if it was alive.

"How long until what?" He could guess what she meant. He just wanted to make her say it. For some reason, he needed her to just spit it out. Gay, how long has he been gay?

"You and Bo. How many nights…how long…just I don't know what I want to know." He could hear tears in her voice, as if he'd caused her heart to break. He resented that she made this about her and her feelings and not about him and his feelings, or Bo's feelings as if they'd done something wrong.

"I'm still the same person you've always known," he said, still looking out the side window at the passing scenery. "Just because I'm—"

"Don't say it, just don't, you're a Marine now, your father was a Marine, you played football, Bo...Bo, oh god, how long?"

He couldn't answer that question. He didn't want to, even if he could. One night or a hundred. There was no answer because he'd always loved Bo. It didn't matter when it became physical.

"I need you to promise me something, okay, Mom? I need you to do one thing for me."

She finally looked at him, her eyes shimmered for a moment. "If I can."

"If something should happen to me—"

"Dylan, no, I don't want to talk about this now." She cut him off and went back to watching the road as if she wasn't the one to bring any of this up.

"Mom, listen to me, okay, for once in your life listen to me. I need you to do one thing for me, that's all." She didn't say anything, she swiped at her left eye but she stayed silent. "If anything happens to me, tell him, okay, in person. He deserves to know firsthand. Not from the news or from some stranger. And not on the phone. Promise me that one thing.

Because I love him. Because I've always loved him."

She turned the radio on, country music poured from the speakers, and the rest of the trip was her being icily silent and him staring out the window as if this wasn't tearing him apart. He'd already lost his dad, now he was losing his mom too. All because she couldn't accept that he could possibly feel something for his best friend. At the airport, he got out and waited by the back for her to pop the hatch open. There was nothing left to say. He was leaving and she was upset about something that he wouldn't change.

"Does he love you?" He stopped at the shouted words and turned to find her about three steps behind him. "Does Bo share your feelings? That's all I'm asking."

"Yes, Mom, he loves me. Maybe it's just stupid high school stuff, maybe it won't last, but this is what it is. I'm gay. And if Bowen Murphy was female I'd have put a ring on his finger before I left him. But I can't. Because this is Florida, and they might not let him play football. His parents don't know. No one knows. Just the three of us. And that's the way we want it. I love him. And I love you. And if anything happens to me. I don't want him left out. He's family, Mom, and I love you both. Just don't leave him out because you can't or won't accept that we could love each other." He shouted, over the sound of cars moving past them, and to cover the sound of his heart breaking. He couldn't look at her, his heart couldn't bear the pain of rejection.

She wrapped her arms around Dylan's neck and held him. Tears burned through his shirt. "I love you. And—I hope I never have to tell him—"

He wrapped his arms around his mother and hugged her tight, "Me either. I hope no one ever has to tell anyone. The war is ending. It'll be fine. It's all just until the Iraqi government can take over and when we get Bin Laden—"

"Don't say it, just don't talk about it. Go have fun, play nice with the other boys. Call when you can." Her voice broke but she held on tight. He didn't want to let her go. After a week of silence, he didn't want to let go.

"I'll be home for Christmas." He knew he lied. And she knew that he lied. She'd been a Marine wife; she knew what he was about to go through, probably better than he did. But she nodded and wiped her eyes. "You'll see."

"Yeah, I'll make a huge turkey."

"Love you, Mom."

"Love you, Dylan. Now hurry or you'll miss your plane."

He walked away with his one suitcase full of the things he couldn't leave behind. Pictures of his mom and dad. And Bo. The shirt Bo had worn the last night he'd seen him. It still had his scent on it. He turned once he was inside the airport, but she was gone.

"See you at Christmas." The station wagon that had hauled him and Bo to many practices receded in the morning light and Dylan wiped the sting of moisture from his eyes. He didn't know which Christmas but he'd keep that promise if it killed him.

Chapter Two

The fucking Super Dome. He stood on the field in the fucking Super Dome. Wearing black and gold. Nothing like it in the world. Even after two years this wasn't old. He could do this forever. But tonight was special. The fucking Super Bowl in the fucking Super Dome and he was part of the home team. The fucking home team. What were the odds of that ever happening? Astronomical, because it had never happened before and Bo was on top of the fucking world.

Six years of working hard. Of taking hits that would have killed a smaller man. Of jumping higher than he'd ever jumped and doing what he never thought he was capable of. This was his reward, he stood in the end zone taking it all in. The show. The big show. The biggest fucking show on the planet. And he was in the middle of it.

The noise grew as the crowd grew. The place was already packed and more people were arriving with every second that passed. Seats were filling, music blaring. On a regular Sunday there was no hearing anything on the field. Even the headset in his helmet was drowned out by the fans. Tonight, he'd be deaf before the end of the game. Guaran-damned-teed.

"Hey, Butterfingers Murphy, you going to catch the ball tonight or stand around with your thumb up your ass like you usually do?" He heard that loud and clear. So did his teammates. They moved in tight as he turned to find the source of the taunt. Every damned hair on his body standing on end.

A trio of Marines stood just past the field goal. They were part of the opening ceremony. Three heroes for the military tribute obviously, all dressed in their dress blues and waiting to go on the field. Big shot heroes. Not so heroic now, were they?

They were supposed to ignore the crowd. Especially assholes trolling for a reaction. But this one he couldn't ignore. Even if he was a Marine. "You think you can do better with some weak ass gun slinging, son, then let's see it." Moving toward the sideline, he dropped his helmet and ignored the hands that pulled him back, slipping out of their grasp in his eagerness to get his hands on the one who dared challenge him.

"Come on, Bo, them's not ordinary Marines, man, them's recon. Didn't you hear about them? And why they're part of the ceremony. You don't fuck with recon, they'll take you down."

He kept moving toward the smart ass who'd called him out. The one standing tall and proud just in front. Almost as if he was at attention. The hard gleam from all three should have warned him. But he was a stupid mother fucker and he got up the loud mouth's face. "Six fucking years and you just show the fuck up without telling me." He didn't care about any god damned thing except getting his arms around him. "Six damned years, Dylan. What the fuck, man?"

Dylan stood ram rod straight, not making a move, not saying a word as Bo shouted at him. He wondered if he'd crossed some line by hugging him when Dylan wrapped his arms around Bo's neck, he was so stiff, so…he felt him breathe out a heavy gasp as he relaxed and held him tight. "I couldn't tell you. I didn't know if I was going to make it until last night. Oh my god, you look so good. You're fucking huge."

"I look good? I'm a big sweaty mess. And you're so damned…the uniform man, so formal and…I missed you so fucking much." He didn't care if he was acting like a baby. He squeezed his friend tight, holding on for dear life.

The crowd seemed to go quiet around him, but he assumed it was because his entire throat had decided to climb inside his ears. "I can't breathe, Bo, and the cameras just found us."

Bo let him go and stepped back, there was no hiding the tears that he couldn't fight off. He didn't even try. He wiped his face, never taking his eyes off his friend out of fear that Dylan would disappear. The idea that this was his one moment to say everything he was thinking and feeling overwhelmed him. "How long are you here for? Please don't say you're leaving right after the game."

"I have a week and then I have to report back." Dylan was in control, no tears, not even a blink or much more than a smile to clue Bo into what he was thinking. He just stood there with the other two, all of them so damned stiff, so hard. Every bit a Marine...a fucking Marine to the core. But Bo could see what he was looking for in his blue eyes. For just a brief moment, Dylan's eyes softened and Bo caught his breath, six long years of hoping that he'd see that look again. And now he knew...nothing had changed. Nothing would change.

"Do you know how much trouble we can get into in a week?" Bo said, hoping like hell that he was spending that week getting into something with Dylan. Or just spend it getting into Dylan.

"I'm counting on it." Dylan stepped up to him and with cameras flashing all around them, hugged him again. "We have a lot of catching up to do after you win this thing."

Bo tuned back into his teammates standing just behind him, their mouths hanging open as they gawked. The noise in the stadium went from low roar to raging cacophony. Reporters, cameras, questions being shouted, lights flashing. It was all surreal. The fucking Super Bowl no longer mattered. All that mattered was making the next week mean something. All of this was now an inconvenience.

"The faster I get this over with then, the better." God, he wanted to kiss him. So damned much.

"You get this over with and we'll go find some trouble. Just like the old days." Dylan shouted over the noise as his teammates came to their senses and started pulling him away from the sideline.

A buzzer sounded, echoing around the dome signaling time for fun was over; Bo had to go in to the locker room. His teammates dragged him away from the trio of Marines and the flashing cameras and reporters shouting questions.

He didn't want to go. "I'm holding you to that. And you're buying the first beer," he shouted over the noise as someone shoved his helmet into his chest.

"You got it," Dylan barked over the screaming and the music playing the Marine Corps Hymn. He lost sight of his friend as he was pushed and pulled into the tunnel leading to the locker room.

"Who's the jarhead, Bocephus, you got a boyfriend in the Corps?" The jokes started before they made it inside. But they all knew not to take it too far.

"Yeah, dickhead, best damned quarterback I ever played with, and he can kill you more ways than you can even imagine." Holy fuck, Dylan was recon, and he'd never once told him. Not once in all of the emails and Skype sessions they'd had over the years. Never. You'd think a person would share something like that with his best damned friend.

"I'm the best quarterback you've ever played with." Came the reply from across the locker room.

Bo smiled because it was mostly true, and because it made Brody crazy when Bo rattled his chain. And a crazy Brody was always a great QB. "Yeah, but you kiss like a fucking girl."

* * * * *

His intention was to keep a low profile. So much for intentions. He hadn't counted on the media or Bo's reaction. But god damn, it felt so damned good to get his arms around the man. Pads and all. He wanted more than a hug. More than a couple of shouted comments that he couldn't remember but weren't what he wanted to say. What he couldn't say. And when he came off the field, the media descended. Officials had hustled him and his fellow Marines through the mess and into a private press box so that he wouldn't have to explain. He'd have to explain enough when he got back. So many regulations forgotten just because Bo couldn't keep his hands to himself. It didn't matter. He'd risk anything to do it all over again. To see him, touch him, smell him. And watching him play, oh yeah, he'd risk the fires of hell just for another chance to watch Bowen Murphy play the game he was born to play.

Hours after the lights in the Super Dome went off and the cameras stopped flashing, he finally felt anonymous. Simply by going back to his hotel and leaving the uniform behind. In jeans and a leather jacket, he looked like just another guy out for a good time after the local team brought home the Lombardi Trophy.

The taxi carried him away from the parties, away from the city, to the address he'd held in his memory for the better part of a year now. Bo's place was far off the beaten path. No city for him. Either of them. Like home. Or something close enough to it.

He paid the driver, giving him something extra to cover the distance, and climbed up the stairs leading to the second floor entrance. The house looked like something out of a movie. Not really big, but expensive to look at and old. The lights outside were soft. No cars sat around to indicate anyone was home. For a moment he worried that Bo would still be talking to reporters but the door opened and Dylan found himself inside and pressed hard against the wood before he could even raise his hand to knock.

"What took you so long?" Bo didn't wait for him to answer before sealing their mouths together. And Dylan melted into him. Six years. More than six years, nearly seven. He wrapped his arms around Bo's neck, letting the big man lift him off his feet. Dylan wrapped his legs around Bo's waist.

"I-came-first-chance-I-could." Was all he could gasp out between kisses, loving the way Bo's hard body fit against his. He traced the defined muscles under the championship t-shirt. The loose nylon shorts Bo wore did nothing to conceal his erection. "Please tell me we're alone?"

"Completely." Bo grasped his ass and hefted him close. Holding him tight as he walked across the room, passing furniture and other rooms. Dylan didn't break eye contact, he didn't even think to protest the handling. He fucking loved the rough handling. Not many men could push him around like he was a doll.

"Fuck, you got big," was all he could think to say when Bo dropped him into the middle of a huge bed. Soft came up to swallow him as hard descended from above him. Sandwiched between heaven and hell, Dylan reached up to trace the line of Bo's chiseled jaw. "I missed you so damned much."

"Kiss now, talk later." Bo crawled over him, pushing at clothes, pulling off shoes and dropping them to the floor. He kept his mouth on Dylan's as if he'd stop breathing if they weren't connected. The rush of blood to parts of his body that made him weak. Rough fingers shoved his jeans down to his knees. Only then did Bo release his mouth to stare down at him. "I might have gotten huge but you're fucking cut now. Look at you. A fucking recon. Baddest of the bad."

Dylan loved the way Bo's hazel gaze caressed his body. Hot molten lava burned in his veins. His dick stood at attention for Bowen. "Fuck now, talk later," he tossed the words back, his voice rougher than he wanted it to be.

Bo flipped him onto his belly and dragged his jeans the rest of the way down his legs. "So damned fucking bad. Look at you, ass in the air, begging like a girl." There was no malice in his words.

Dylan shoved his ass higher at the taunt. "At least I can get it up. Are you going to fuck or talk all night?" Dylan didn't bat an eye when Bo pulled a ribbon of condoms from beneath the pillow along with a bottle of lube. Six years was a long time to be celibate. A long fucking time. He didn't want to know. It didn't matter. Cold gel slithered down his crack, hot fingers rubbed it in, going deep enough that Dylan forgot all about the condoms and the lube and just moved. "I missed you."

The sound of a condom wrapper tearing and the scent of latex filled his senses. Bo leaned over him, his mouth grazing Dylan's ear just as the blunt head of his cock pushed into him.

"Missed you so damned much. Want to keep you here forever."

Dylan grunted when Bo pressed him into the mattress, his balls now flush against Dylan's ass. They lay still, just breathing, adjusting. "You can keep me just like this for one week."

"Naked and impaled. God damn that is probably the sexiest damn tattoo I've ever seen." Teeth scraped the bulldog tat on his shoulder. Bo moaned and bit into him, making him moan and slam his body back into the giant pinning him to the bed.

"Worship the ink later. Make me come, now. Fuck you smell so good."

"I stink but thanks for noticing." Bo flexed his hips, moving slowly, so torturously slowly. "I didn't shower. I didn't want to take the time."

"Super Bowl sweat, smells good to me." Dylan twisted underneath him until he could wrap an arm around Bo's neck. He dragged the band away that held Bo's hair back, allowing long sweaty tendrils to fall over him. "Six years, are you going to cut it now?" He ran his hand through the mane, touching it for the first time ever.

"When you can come home to stay. I'll cut it then." The hair thing started the first time Dylan had managed to have a five minute Skype session with him after boot camp. His hair gone, much too both their dismay. Hell, Dylan didn't know that losing his hair would bother him so much. He sure as hell wasn't prepared for Bo's reaction. In the end, Bo had sworn he'd grow his for the both of them.

"If I told you not to."

"Then I'll keep it long." Bo pulled out of him with a gasp and Dylan found himself on his back with blond hair hanging over his face. He pulled his legs back and accepted his lover into him with an arch of his back and a sigh. Dylan wound his hands in the long sweaty mess and pulled Bo's mouth down for a wet sloppy kiss.

"Fuck me, Mr. MVP, show me what you got." Dylan wanted everything he'd missed in the last six years and he wanted it now. He wrapped his arms and legs around his friend and moved with him. Setting a rhythm that had Bo's eyes rolling. Sweat slicked them both, making it hard to keep his grip. Long, heavily muscled arms scooped him from below and somehow Bo was on his knees with Dylan wrapped around him. There was no room between them for anything but sweat. He hooked his ankles as Bo gripped his hips, changing the pace. Rougher, faster, adrenaline pumping between them. Years to make up for.

"Fuck yeah, gonna blow, Bo. Now." He laughed, finding the ridge along Bo's shoulder to bite down as his body went rock hard.

He lay quietly in Bo's arms, arms and legs leaden and heavy, his heart beating harder and faster than even the worst days of training. A soft chuckle accompanied the swipe of a long slim hand over the back of his shaved head.

"Oo-fucking-rah," Bo said, his voice was choked with more than just exertion.

Dylan caught Bo's lips and held him close. Next week would come too soon, right now he couldn't get close enough. "Oorah," he agreed moving slowly while Bo emptied himself into Dylan's body, his groans turned to tears that Dylan kissed away. "Oorah."

Chapter Three

"Are you hungry?" Bo lay in Dylan's arms, head on his shoulder, arm draped over his belly, holding him for fear that he'd leave if he let him go. Dylan raked a hand through his just washed hair. His stomach rose and fell in a steady rhythm but he wasn't asleep.

"I could eat. Are you?" Dylan continued to pet him, humming softly every now and then.

"Yes. Didn't get anything after the game."

"I'm surprised you managed to get out of the stadium in one piece. So damned proud of you. You just snatched that ball out of the air like it was nothing. By one point, damn, Bo, so fucking close."

"Skin of my teeth. I knew you were watching. I was showing off."

"You were always a show off. Now you're a god."

"And you're a hero. I heard some of what the announcers were saying about the three of you. It was loud down in the tunnel but I heard it. Why didn't you ever tell me you were Special Forces?" He didn't know why it hurt to be left out like that. They'd never kept secrets, not even across the distance and years. Except this one.

"For the record, I'm not Force Recon, not really. I'm MARSOC, specifically MEU Marine Expeditionary Unit, promoted to Staff Sergeant last month and I'm out of Camp Lejeune. I got special leave to be here. I deploy to Afghanistan next week."

Bo rolled over onto his stomach, resting his chin on his lover's pectoral to stare into his eyes. He didn't know what he was searching for. The boy he remembered behind the hard eyes and sculpted body, maybe? He traced a scar that wasn't there the last time they'd lain like this together. A long jagged scar that ran across his sternum.

"I don't know what most of that means. So not Recon?"

"Sort of the super sneaky branch of Recon now. I've worked hard to get this promotion out of regular Recon."

"So super sneaky military shit? Damn, Dyl, maybe I shouldn't ask anything more." Because his imagination was enough, the reality of what Dylan did for a living would tear him apart. It would be like that day all those years ago with him, begging his friend to unenlist.

"I appreciate that." Dylan took his hand, twining their fingers together before he kissed Bo's knuckles. "Promotion or no promotion, I'm out in a little more than a year. Eight years and I'm done."

Bo digested that piece of information. Nodding, trying not to read anything in while hoping for the best. "Any idea what you want to do when you get out?"

"Sleep. Get fat. I don't know. Haven't thought about it. Beyond finding you and getting you naked, after that I'll figure it out." Dylan rolled him onto his back and took over the leaning on position. "I want to be where you are. Unless that's a problem." There was uncertainty in his eyes. And maybe a touch of fear.

Bo traced his bottom lip with his thumb. "I'll have to let my harem go. All those ball boys will just have to get over me."

"God, I hope you're keeping it legal, wouldn't want you being someone's prison bitch before I get back here to make you mine." That touch of uncertainty turned to something else. A flash of jealousy maybe.

"Nobody's made me their bitch yet. Not from lack of trying. But I'm holding on to my bitch." Sounded stupid and he winced. "There have been guys, Dylan. I'm not going to lie to you. Nameless faceless fucks. Nobody I want to bring home to meet the parents."

Dylan crawled over his body, straddling him. His nose touched Bo's and those hard eyes seemed to chill him to the bone. "I didn't expect you to stay chaste all this time. It's not fair."

"And you?" Bo didn't know why he wanted to know. Glutton for punishment. Just the thought of Dyl being with anyone like this ate at him. But what he'd said, six years was too long to go without sex.

"Nothing like this, but not exactly nameless or faceless. Straight guys mostly. No one has my heart. Just you."

He wriggled down Bo's body, god, he was perfect, not small, not like the last guy who blew him. Dylan was a big man. Six foot. Broad. Huge fucking arms. Arms that appeared small wrapped in Bo's hand. And he held his arms while Dylan licked his cock like a Popsicle. First, running his tongue up from the root to catch the dripping goodness, and then swirling it around the tip before swallowing him whole.

"Straight guys don't give head like that." Bo arched off the bed in surprise. The first time Dylan had gone down on him it had been sloppy and clumsy and Bo had come in his mouth about two minutes in. Dylan had gagged and spit it all out. "Hate that you do that so damned well."

Dylan eased off and laughed, "I can stop."

"Fuck no, suck me, Jarhead. And this time you better fucking swallow my load." He gripped the base of his cock and slapped it against Dylan's lips. Dylan opened on the second slap and sucked him inside. Just the tip. He licked the top, tongue delving into the slit. Wicked eyes stared up at him, promising him sin and redemption and so much more. Experience stared up at him. And Bo gave himself over to the man his love had become. "Please," he whispered, ignoring the pain that slashed through his heart. "Please."

Dylan's eyes changed, something that appeared strangely like sadness entered the pale depths. He took him deep, down his throat. There was no gagging and nothing sloppy. Bo fell back onto his pillow, one hand behind Dylan's head, mostly for the contact, and lost his mind. Fucking into him, down his throat, he cried his name, begged for more, and to stop, but Dylan didn't stop until Bo shoved his heels into the bed and arched his hips, coming, hard. He couldn't stop and Dylan took it all.

"Is that what the military teaches nowadays? Maybe I should join up," he said when he could feel his tongue again. "I think I bit a hole in my tongue. Fuck. Oh fuck, Dylan."

"After that, Bo shouldn't be thinking about fucking. He shouldn't be able to think at all." Dylan settled on top of him, blue eyes sparkling with satisfaction as he stared down. "Bo should say thank you, Dylan."

"Best head ever. Thank you, Dylan." Bo pulled him tight and kissed him. "Best night of my life."

"I guess winning the Super Bowl all by your lonesome would account for best night status."

For a moment Bo simply stared at him. "That was tonight? I think maybe you did short circuit my brain." Another slow kiss that tasted of spunk and Dylan. "Can we get food now?"

"God, yes, I was hoping you'd remember that." Dylan rolled off him and searched around for his jeans while Bo tried to catch his breath. "So what does Bo Murphy eat now that he's famous?"

"Everything I can get my hands on. Anything that won't eat me first." He found his shorts on the floor and followed Dylan from the bedroom into the main house. He watched the way Dyl's hips moved in the tight jeans. His mouth going dry as he studied the tattoos on his back. "You have my name down your spine." The letters were swirled into other designs that Bo couldn't make out in the semi dark.

Dylan turned to face him, his eyes inscrutable. "Is that okay?"

"Why wouldn't it be okay?" Bo stopped short, his mind still sluggish after the blow job. "Why would it bother me?"

"Because, I don't know, I wanted you with me. If I can't be with you then I have you on me. I was still a kid when I got that one." For a moment the hardened Marine gave way to the boy Bo remembered. But only for a moment. "I get shit from the guys about it. But they get it even if they don't know how deep my love for you is. Brothers, we were brothers. I just don't want you to think I'm looking for something that you're not comfortable with."

"And if I get a matching one with your name down my back would you be okay with that?" Bo asked, the idea taking hold now. He'd never inked his body while his teammates did. Not that he had a problem with it. Nothing ever meant that much to him to make it a part of him. Except Dylan, and he didn't know if Dylan would want him to take that step.

"You'll risk outing yourself to have my name on your back? It's football, man, not the military. You know how homophobic some of those guys are." Dylan stood in front of him. Arms up and over his shoulders. He gazed up the two inches he needed to see into Bo's eyes. His heart shining in the blue depths for Bo to see.

"And the military is so open and accepting now that Don't Ask Don't Tell is gone? I know you take shit from the homophobes, brothers or no brothers."

"Actually they thought I was a crazy stalker fan. No one believed that I knew you. Okay except for the few who managed to get in on our Skype sessions, god, you don't know how much I wanted to tell you all those times."

"Tell me what?" Bo felt the wall behind his back, it was cold and unmoving. The body in front of him hot and unyielding. His brain finally possibly fizzled out and his dick took over the thinking.

"How much I really missed you. How much you meant to me. How much I wanted to be with you. How much I wanted to suck your dick. How much I loved you. That if we were different we could get married. Maybe have a couple of kids or dogs or something. That I'd die for you." The words were accompanied by kisses. More sweet kisses, on his nose, his cheeks, his eyelids, finally his lips. "And not because you can catch a football. Or because you're gorgeous. But because I remember when you couldn't catch anything, and when you were an awkward ugly kid trying to grow into his hands and feet. I loved you even before you were sex on legs."

"This week is going to kill me, isn't it?" Bo whispered against his lover's mouth, his body trembled under Dylan's expert hands.

"We have nearly seven years to make up for. And then another year to store up for. So yeah, I'm taking no prisoners."

"I have things to do today. Or I'll lose my job."

"You might want to set an alarm or something. Or we'll just stay up all night so you don't forget." Dylan sucked at his neck, pulling up a hickey Bo wouldn't be able to explain come morning. But he didn't care, he returned the favor.

"I'll take you with me. Show you off. And when I'm finished there, we'll move you back here. Can't believe you even checked into a hotel in the first place."

"And ruin the best surprise in the history of ever. Your face, oh it was priceless, at first you were all big man pissed off, and then you were this big puppy dog. I wanted to kiss you right there on the field. All those cameras. I couldn't but I wanted to." Dylan's hands roamed low over his body and that's all Bo heard. The part about kissing. And he dragged Dylan in for another long slow kiss. Clothes that were hastily donned were slowly divested. Food forgotten again. So many body parts that needed tasting, so little time.

* * * * *

He stood on the forty yard line holding a football that he'd snagged from an equipment stand. Years flew away and he was a kid again when practice was the only thing he knew. Practice and school. Get up in the morning before the other kids. Be on the field before the sun was even up. Throw hard and fast. Connect with Bo at the other end of the field. Do it again. And again. And again. For years. Bo was fast back then. Really fast. Big boys like him weren't usually fast. He liked to eat and always carried a bit of a spare tire around his waist, but he could run. And he could jump. And he could eat. He could still eat. But now he worked out all the time or he wouldn't have the body to make him a world class athlete.

His freaking arms had to be registered lethal weapons.

Dylan remembered everything from those years. He had a lot of time to play those days over in his mind. Long lonely nights to get through. He felt old. Sometimes. At twenty-four almost twenty-five. He felt so old. And alone.

Bo was inside somewhere doing secret football things that didn't include him. The day-after meetings and whatever they did in the big leagues. Most likely taking some serious heat for the picture on the front page of the newspaper this morning. The two of them locked in embrace, tears in Bo's eyes. Dylan tried so damned hard not to break down when the first tear fell from Bo's eye. He wanted to. He could see the shimmer in his own eyes splashed right there on the front page. The feel good homecoming story. Football hero and war hero together again.

With Bo winning the Super Bowl with four touchdown runs out of the five scored, last night was his night. And Dylan was there for it. The most perfect night in the history of his life. Being there when Bo did everything Bo said he was going to do. And knowing at least one of those salutes in the end zone was for Dylan. The last one. The one when Bo pointed to the heavens with the ball in his hand. That was his move back in the day.

"Hey, Jarhead, sling me that football." The shout came from a hallway at the far end of the field and Dylan jumped. He hadn't expected anyone would mind him being out on the practice field but he wasn't supposed to be there. Regulations were regulations. Bo and a couple of other men emerged from the shadows. Dylan couldn't recognize them, not without their uniforms with names emblazoned on their backs. They were just men in sweats or jeans. Not football gods. Dylan didn't stop to think, he dropped into his stance took two steps back and let the ball fly over the field to the man who'd challenged him to throw it.

Bo ran forward and with the gracefulness of a ballet dancer he put himself in the air and snagged the ball, landing as if no time had ever parted them and this was just another day of practice. He held the ball in one huge hand, grinning from ear to ear as he jogged over the field.

"Wow, it's like you do that for a living or something." Dylan felt stupid if Bo hadn't made a run for it, the throw would have fallen way short.

"What was that, sixty yards or so?" Bo came to a stop not far from him and tossed the ball back into his hands. "If I hadn't jumped for it, it would have gone another ten maybe fifteen yards." There was awe in his voice. "Do it again. Once is just a fluke."

Dylan glanced over to where the other players stood watching. More emerged from the hallway into the indoor practice field. "No, man, it was just a fluke. It would have fallen short."

"Bullshit, you've still got an arm. Let's see it. Just like we used to do. Last play of the state championship. Do it." Bo ordered and took off at a full run. Dylan watched the denim encased muscles in his legs work to move him that fast. He realized Bo was running the exact play he'd run for that game, and again without thinking he stepped back and arced the ball through the air. Bo made it to the end zone and zigged to the right, turning just in time for the ball to drop into his hands. No muss, no fuss. Bo screaming in the end zone made him blush. Marines don't blush and that's just all there was to it.

"Don't make me come down there and hurt you, Bowen, I will. And it won't be pretty." He shouted over the ruckus his lover made. But that just called even more attention to them.

"You'd have to catch me first. And that is not something you could ever do. Stick to throwing long bombs." Bo, holding the football in one hand, taunted him with it, pointing as if this was just another practice and it was just them fooling around.

Maybe Dylan couldn't catch him, at least not back in the day, but Bo didn't know him now. Dylan took off at a dead run. He usually did this loaded down with a good fifty pounds, more often closer to seventy or eighty. Chasing Bo down wouldn't be a problem anymore. He was across the field before Bo had a chance to think of an escape, and with ease he lifted the bigger man off his feet and put him on the ground.

Crowing. "Oo-fucking-rah."

Bo just stared up at him before the grin spread over his face. "That was amazing. You're still not as fast as me, but damned close, only because my legs are longer maybe. What the fuck do they feed you in the Marines?"

"Humiliation and motivation to get our fat asses up that hill. Twenty miles, with enough weaponry and supplies, in the heat and the rain. While you princesses have it easy." Dylan climbed to his feet and held his hand out to help Bo up. He didn't expect him to take it, he didn't expect him to grin that shit-eater grin of his that said he was up to no good either. And he sure as fuck didn't expect to be thrown over Bo's shoulder and run across the field like he weighed nothing.

"You were saying, Princess?" Bo dropped him on his feet back in the middle of the field. He wasn't even winded. "Might not be a fucking Marine but I ain't no lightweight."

A whistle blew from somewhere off to the side. Bo jumped and for a moment his face went panicky. Last time Dylan had seen that look on his face was the morning his mother had walked in on them, naked and kissing and maybe a couple of other interesting things going on too but he couldn't be sure just how long she'd been there. This time Dylan was absolutely one hundred percent sure that they'd done nothing to make anyone think they were more than they said they were.

"Bocephus! Who's your friend?" The voice sounded more like one of the drill sergeants back at base than any coach Dylan remembered. Looked like one too, had the bearing and the haircut and the take no prisoners mean ass stare.

Dylan pulled himself to attention. "Staff Sergeant Dylan Sunday, Sir." He didn't salute. But only because he knew Bo would never let him forget it if he had. The grin that broke out on the man's face said he'd scored some serious points.

"Sempre Fi." The coach took the ball from Bo's hands. "That's quite an arm you got there, son, where did you play?"

"Big Bend High School, Florida, Sir. Same place this knucklehead matriculated from." Dylan wondered just how much trouble he'd caused Bo when the ball ended up back in his hands.

"No, son, I mean what college did you attend? But I'm going to guess you and that glorious arm didn't get picked up back in Florida."

"No, sir, I'm on my second enlistment. Went in straight out of high school." This was something he didn't go around telling but somehow he knew this guy would understand.

"Sometimes that's the way it is. Some give some. Let me see that play again. 'Cephus, get your ass downfield, fast as your legs can get you there." Dylan let the unfinished and some give all run through his head for a moment before shaking it off.

Bo didn't ask a question; he didn't make a sound. He simply dropped his shoulders, bent his knees and took off like a flash. When he was at the thirty yard line Dylan pulled the ball up, stepped back and threw with all his might. The ball spiraled up and over the green turf, and then just when it looked like Dylan had overshot his target, Bo zigged again and was in the right place at the right time to meet the ball. Those glorious muscles of his bunched and moved as he jumped to get his hands on it, and then he landed and started back to the coach.

"Bet that gimmick won you a couple of games." The coach said holding the ball as he signaled to the sidelines and three guys ran out.

"State championship." Bo slapped Dylan on the back. "Best and I mean BEST quarterback I've ever worked with."

"Don't let Brody hear you say that," the coach answered with a malicious grin and started calling off plays, he handed the ball to the center and moved back while Dylan stood there trying to decide how much longer he was going to let this farce go on. Obviously a lot longer. He assumed the position behind the center, and when the ball snapped, he watched as the two receivers took off down the field running intricate patterns meant to confuse the defense. He took his time and picked his receiver then sent the ball barreling down the field. Not a high arc but a straight out bullet to land in the other receiver's hands. Knocking him backward from the force.

"Oh fuck me, that hurt." The guy rubbed his chest where there should have been pads. A huge grin on his face. "Yeah, baby. Damn."

The coach just stood there looking angry. Hand on one hip, the other in front of his mouth.

"There's not much to do in the desert. Work out and kill people. Football is still football no matter the turf," he explained while the two receivers made their way back. Bo's grin fading as he came closer.

By now they'd attracted a serious audience. Suits as well as players moved around or sat in the small set of stands. The coach standing beside him didn't say a thing; he called in one of the secondary quarterbacks and put Dylan in Bo's place.

"Sit it out, 'Cephus, let me see what your buddy can do without you egging him on." And Bo went over to the sidelines without saying one word. But then this was his coach, he would just have to blindly follow orders. Figures, *now* Bo followed orders.

"Uh, sir, I uh, really this is not necessary. I'm not sure what's going on but—"

"Just shut up and run, ask questions later," he said in the drill sergeant voice and Dylan did exactly what he was told despite his own rank and years away from basic. So he ran, and when the quarterback called the play he ran instinctively, ending up in the end zone before the other receiver, the ball in his hands and he'd had to jump to get it.

Whistles from the sidelines broke the quiet. The clapping started with Bo and spread through the crowd. What the hell was that fool doing anyway? Showing off. The answer came to him. Hurricane Bowen was a force of nature. Always had been and always would be. And he was just being himself.

"Damn, 'Cephus, your boyfriend throws better, runs faster, and jumps higher than you do. What's he like in bed, and I might just marry him?" Someone shouted from one on the sidelines. Dylan knew it was bullshit. But the comment still made Dylan flush, mostly with anger.

"Shut up, Pisshead, I'm getting his name tattooed on my ass because he just owned me." Bo pushed the other guy, only a little, but the other guy was not as big as Bo so he teetered a bit before he caught himself. There was laughing and slapping and shoving.

"Yeah, well, we get a diamond ring because of you so we'll keep it a secret. Big fucking Super Bowl ring. And 'Cephus has a Recon boyfriend." The guy made a zipping motion across his lips before he shoved Bo back. Bo gazed across the field and smiled. Everything here was good. Bo was good.

The coach had made his way down the field to where Dylan stood alone, trying not to let the ribbing get his hackles up. "They're just messing with him. The newspaper picture was already a major source of embarrassment to him in the locker room. Being caught with tears was not something his ego could stand. I did some checking and found out you weren't supposed to be in that ceremony last night."

"I wanted to be here for him. And I wanted him to know I was here and not some anonymous face up in the cheap seats." Dylan didn't like having to explain himself. "I haven't seen him since he left for college his freshman year. Hell, this is the first time I've been stateside in nearly two years. Always missed connections. I'm home when he's in the middle of play offs or training camp or finals. It's been a hell of a long time. Missed him so damned much." He realized he'd said more than he should have and shut his mouth.

"Know the feeling well. That was me a decade or so ago. Listen, kid, I'm going to ask you one question: are you career?" The coach lost the drill instructor and the coach voice and became just another Marine.

"I have one year, six months and twenty days left and I'm out." He watched Bo on the sideline and nodded. One year, six months and twenty days, that's all he had left to give his country before he could come home to his reward.

"You made plans yet?" This seemed more than just casual curiosity but Dylan wouldn't allow himself to entertain any ideas that the coach might be making any offers. Not one at all.

"Get drunk, get laid, not ever wear anything in the brown or tan family ever again. Not much after that. Maybe go to school. Maybe become a beach bum. My opportunities are wide open at this moment." It didn't do him any good to dream about those days until he made it home again in one piece and mostly sane. If he could manage those last two things, he'd be golden. After that he'd figure it out.

"Just don't get killed and call me when you're ready. It'll be late in the summer, the season will most likely be started, but I'll see what I can do for you. You've got talent. Raw, to be sure, but that arm needs to be in the NFL." He extended a business card at the same time that an arm snaked around Dylan's neck.

Dylan didn't stop to think where he was or that there would most likely be no threat. He flipped his aggressor over his shoulder and buried his knee in the guy's neck. Hand going to the knife he kept strapped to his leg just above his boot. Bo's ghostly pale face and terrified eyes penetrated the haze, and he didn't pull his jeans leg up. Standing quickly, he pulled Bo to his feet.

"Don't do that, man, okay? Just don't. I can kill you. And I don't think your owners would appreciate that too much."

He didn't reach for the card. He just stood there trying to act like this was normal. That he didn't just freak out in front of civilians.

"Fuck, Dyl, you just outran me in fucking combat boots. You have got to be shitting me." The sound of laughter was all that Dylan could remember after that. The coach who turned out to be Dale Shannon, the offensive coordinator, put the card in his jacket pocket and slapped him on the back.

"Something to think on, kid, maybe I'll see you back here in two years' time. Until then give 'em hell."

"I'll do that, sir."

"Show's over. You'd think you lot would have something better to do the day after you won the fucking Super Bowl. Don't you have people to be celebrating with? Or we can start working on next year's—" Shannon shouted out and people started to scramble before this became real work.

"Come on, Rambo, you have a tattoo to buy me. And I need some pointers on that over the shoulder takedown thing you got going on. Wonder if it's legal in the NFL… Who the hell cares? It was wicked. Just thanks for not pulling the knife." Bo punched him on the shoulder and laughed as they walked from the training area to his truck.

"Sorry about that, I'm usually more in control." Dylan turned the radio from the rock station to a country station, because he knew that Bo didn't mind, just to get his mind off the fool he'd made of himself.

"Nothing to be sorry for. Just, you know, when we get home, I'm going to want to be thrown over your shoulder caveman style and maybe you can hold me down and stick other things in me. I promise not to fight too hard." Bo put the truck in reverse, and before he backed out, he reached over and grabbed Dylan's gearstick too. "Just so we're clear on what I want stuck in me. Okay? This bad boy right here. Not the pig sticker."

"Yes, sir," Dylan said, feeling the flush come on again. This time though, he knew exactly why he was turning red. And it had a lot to do with Bo's hand on his dick. In public.

"Now that's what I'm talking about. And you can call me sir while you're fucking me. I just got all kinds of horny." He laughed and hit the gas, burning rubber to get out of the parking lot just as fast as he could. Because the day was wasting and there was fucking to be done.

Dylan put the card in his wallet without letting Bo see it. He'd think about that later. When he could see a future that didn't involve desert sand and bloodshed.

Chapter Four

"I am so going to fuck you up, six ways from Sunday, Sunday," Bo moaned as he leaned over the dashboard. His back burned like a million tiny bees decided to use him for a pin cushion.

"How is this my fault, Murphy? You're the one who decided to get a tattoo. I didn't tell you to. In fact, I do recall telling you that the spine is probably not the best place to get your first one but you had to be bad ass and do it anyway." Dylan glanced over at him as they drove through town. Bo was thrilled that he didn't smirk—too much.

"I wasn't nearly drunk enough for that. You should have talked louder. Something. This shit hurts."

"You only bled a little bit and there's hardly no swelling. You're just being a baby."

"Oh yeah? Well, how drunk were you when you got yours?" He wanted desperately to rub something in after the hosing back at the practice field.

Dylan didn't say anything; he just stared ahead and tapped his thumbs on the steering wheel as he navigated based on the GPS's directions.

"I don't fucking believe you. You had to be drunk or something to deal with that kind of…shit. You're a masochist, aren't you? You like pain. You get off on pain. That's it. I knew it."

"I wanted it to mean something. Both of them. I went in sober so I wouldn't walk away with a dead chicken or dancing mermaid or something stupid. Both of mine mean something to me. Especially the one down my spine."

Bo sat quietly for a long time, watching the winter scenery pass him by. They were out of the city and into the quiet of bayou country now. "You mean something to me. And not just as a guy I'd like to fuck on a regular basis either. I mean, you came back and we picked up right where we left off. You're fun. And you get me. You let me get away with shit no one else will tolerate. I've always liked that about you."

"You like that because I was letting you get away with the same shit I was trying to get away with. There's a fine line between love and enabling in our relationship if you think about it long enough. And that's the liquor talking. Next you'll be on the floor sobbing and saying I love you, man."

"But I do love you. You're my man. My—I have no idea what we are. What are we?"

"I see us sort of as a modern day Fred and Barney." Dylan answered in all seriousness. Bo must have made a face because Dylan reached over and squeezed his knee. "Okay no, Scooby and Shaggy? But I'm not sure if I'm comfortable with being either one. How about Ken and GI Joe. You're my Ken doll. When Ken let his hair grow out long and played football and realized that cheerleader Barbie was all boobs and no dick."

"You are seriously messed up in the head. You know that, right?" Bo leaned back, wincing as the seat put too much pressure on the tender line down his back. "I was thinking more the macho, sports-type figures. Of—"

"Name me two macho sports-type figures that were doing each other and I'll decide if I want to compared to either one." Dylan turned onto the long drive that led up to Bo's house while Bo thought about the pop culture role models in his life. He couldn't think of one gay sports figure, much less two. Or even two figures that had a natural symbiotic relationship to compare them to.

"We're unique. That's a first. I've never been unique in anything I've ever done."

"Bullshit." Dylan stopped the truck in front of Bo's house and turned to face him. "You're a six foot three, two hundred fifty pound exasperating person who is nothing but unique. Valedictorian, Bowen. You were the fucking valedictorian and you play football. You went to college on an academic scholarship instead of a sports scholarship. And you graduated. With honors. While playing football. While winning football games. While staying clean and sober and not knocking up a cheerleader or a beauty queen."

"I wouldn't exactly say sober. Especially right now. And that last part is only because I'm gay and wouldn't be swayed by any evil breasted cheerleader. Okay, there was that one guy, I'm pretty sure he wanted to fuck me, but I'm not going to let some pushy guy who might go squealing that Bo likes dick while he's got his hand up some girl's skirt, get in my pants."

"And you sort of flame when you're mostly drunk. I should have figured out a hell of a lot sooner those times when we managed to get beer and not get caught. You giggled." Dylan smiled, his eyes sparkling with amusement at Bo's expense, which made Bo angry.

"I did not giggle." Bo giggled. "Oh fuck, I giggle. And it's funny as shit."

"You giggle and it's sexy as shit. You were big and tough and kept the bullies off me when I was short and fat.

And I've always found you to be the most unique person I've ever met. You're not a hard ass and you're not a doormat. You're a decent human being, and that, my friend, is unique in the world of football." The amused gleam left his eyes, replaced by something a little more violent that sent a thrill down Bo's newly tattooed spine.

"I am so going to go all Fred Flintstone on your ass when we get inside." Bo lost his train of thought just listening to Dylan talk. "You have the sexiest damn voice. Makes me want to do bad things to you."

"Oh, no, baby, not this time. This time I'm Fred and you're Barney and you are going to bend over for me. I'm going to fuck me a Super Bowl champion." His voice went deeper than Bo had ever heard him speak before. Deep, seductive, and oh so fucking, yeah, Bo had a hard-on for Dylan's voice. Yes, please, everything he just said. Now.

"You are? Who? You think he'll let me in on that because that would be really awesome." In his haste to get out of the truck and into position for exactly what Dylan promised, Bo reached for the door handle and missed. "Dyl? It occurs to me that I might be drunk."

"It occurs to me that you drank a fifth of Jack while you were under the needle. And if you weren't drunk then this wouldn't be funny as hell."

"Dammit, Fred, you are just an awful friend. I'm going to go tell Wilma that you won't let me fuck the Super Bowl champion. Okay, wait...Shaggy and Scooby? Seriously? You think Shaggy and Scooby were doing it?" Bo had to wonder if this was the alcohol talking or if his friend was seriously messed up in the head.

"Shaggy was a stoner who thought the dog talked. He didn't seem interested in either of the girls and he didn't seem interested in Freddie... So yes, I would have to say that Shaggy and Scooby had a sexual relationship," Dylan said in all seriousness. He didn't even crack a smile.

"I just can't picture Shaggy—you know..." There was no way he was going to say it, or even make the hand symbols or acknowledge this ridiculous conversation.

"I always thought of Shaggy as more of a bottom." Dylan grinned and let himself out his side of the truck. Bo just sat there, wondering how he'd missed that Dylan was crazy. He watched as his friend walked around the front of the truck, twirling the keys on his trigger finger and whistling.

"You are not exactly sane, are you?" He fell out of the truck into Dylan's arms. The whistling continued, the theme to Scooby-doo. Sadistic masochistic asshole. "Are you going to kill me in my sleep?"

"Maybe just a little." Dylan helped him stand and kept an arm around him as Bo stumbled up the stairs. "Because you're too drunk to fuck right now. So I have to find something to keep me entertained while you sober up."

That made sense. Dyl always needed something to keep his hands busy. When he was bored, that's when they got into trouble. "Remember the year we dug a crater in my backyard. We said we were looking for dinosaur fossils but all we did was break a water pipe. Oh, man, I thought your dad and my dad were going to take turns skinning us alive."

"You got a pool out of it, so it wasn't all bad. We never did find any fossils. And that's why they put us in football in the first place." Dylan fumbled with the keys looking for the right one for the door.

"To keep us from digging up the front yard." Bo remembered that summer and after three days of his parents raising hell about how much damage two unsupervised nine years could wreak, his mom had laughed and said, *"Why the hell not just go ahead and put in the pool we keep talking about. Maybe they'll leave the front yard alone."*

"To keep us busy. To wear us out. So that we would come home at the end of the day and fall asleep over our hamburgers instead of run around in the street all night. It was the best thing they could have done. Well, maybe I could have lived without the whipping. But that's it." Dylan dumped him unceremoniously on the sofa in the sparse living room. And followed him down. "You weigh a fucking ton."

"You're just a light weight." Bo swiveled in the seat and put his head on Dylan's leg, he propped his feet up on the other arm and kicked off his shoes. "Sorry I'm drunk."

"I'm not. Okay, yeah, that you're drunk and I'm not going to get laid any time soon, but you're a happy drunk. I enjoy you this way. Walking down memory lane with you. Playing with you. I'm so happy just being here and having you look at me like you are right now." Dylan touched Bo's nose with the tip of a finger then traced it along Bo's lips. "I'm glad that the grown up you is still a lot like the boy I left behind."

And that's when Bo's heart threatened to quit. Those words that had stayed with him all these years. He'd been the one left behind. "I thought I was doing the leaving and it tore me apart. I begged my parents to do something to help you pay for school. I tried to talk the coaches, everyone into helping you get something."

Dylan sighed wearily. "We had different paths to walk, Bo. I'm just happy that we can cross paths again and be who we were. Gives me something to look forward to when I'm ready to stop walking the one I'm on now," he said, running his fingers through Bo's hair, pulling a long strand up to rub between his fingers.

"I'll be here when you're ready. We'll see if we can walk the same path then. I think we can." Bo reached up to trace the frown lines around Dylan's mouth. "I want to be with you."

"Right now, I'd like lunch and a nap. Because you kept me up all night and I have jetlag and then maybe we'll stay up all night again." He pushed Bo onto the floor, all sympathy and goodwill gone now that his stomach was involved. Bo climbed unsteadily to his feet and followed him into the kitchen.

"Food I got. And a bed for napping. But it's going to cost you." He caught Dylan in front of the fridge and pinned him to the front of it. Leaning in, he rubbed his nose to Dylan's. "A kiss.

Because I can't get enough of kissing you."

"All I have to do is kiss you and you'll feed me?" Dylan pushed Bo's hair back over his ears and pulled the elastic holder out so that the rest of his hair hung loose. Bo felt for all the world like he was being petted. Petted and loved. Instead of worshipped. He never wanted that part of the bargain. Play some ball, have some fun, that's what he wanted.

"Yeah, funny how that works," he lowered his lips, slicking his tongue against Dylan's lips while the pale late afternoon sun bathed them through the windows. "Make me happy and I'll make you happy."

Dylan opened his mouth and Bo slid his tongue inside, tasting him. Savoring him. Taking his time. Before he was finished exploring Dylan's mouth, the tight body beneath him demanded more, more in the form of grinding and humping that left them both breathless and sticky. Dylan went over first, crying into Bo's mouth, pleasure, sharp, fast, electric zapped him when Dylan's orgasm took him and Bo followed him over. Right there in the kitchen, fully dressed, but he wouldn't stop the kiss. He needed it to go on forever. Dylan's hands in his hair and down his back into his jeans told him how much he agreed. Lunch could wait. This couldn't. He didn't care if the entire state of Louisiana was outside that damned window. Dylan was his for only a week and he was going to make every second of that week count. Starting with getting out of cum-soaked pants.

He tugged at Dylan's jeans, pulling the buttons free and pushing until the material stopped at his knees. He followed, going down on his knees as Dylan pulled his shirt over his head to expose all that tanned skin that made Bo's mouth dry and his brain stop working. He kissed the line of hair down Dylan's belly. The scent of cum strong, musky, he wanted to taste. Dylan groaned at the first touch of his tongue.

He leaned back to show him the thick line of fluid before he swallowed.

Dylan's eyes went dark, his knees trembled. "You gonna suck me, cowboy?"

"Yeehaw," Bo answered, sliding his tongue through the goo around Dylan's navel, licking until he'd cleaned that much up. When he was finished, he turned his attention to Dyl's cock, still dripping pearl-colored fluid. "You smell so fucking good, I just want to…" He didn't finish. Instead, he showed his friend exactly what he wanted by closing his mouth over his cock and licking every bit of flavor from him.

"Bo, oh god damn, fuck," Dylan grabbed a fist full of hair with one hand and reached over his head to hold onto the top of the refrigerator with the other. Bo smiled around the thick head and swallowed him as deeply as he could. Sucking as he went. He watched Dylan. His heart pounding in his chest at the sight of his lover trying to stay in control. And failing. He took the first thrust, relaxing his jaws to take the next. Dylan fucked into him, while Bo held onto his hips encouraging him to move, encouraging his moans and curses. He wanted Dylan to lose complete control. And with a cry that echoed around the open kitchen, Dylan did just that. Cum, savory and a little salty filled Bo's mouth.

Bo palmed his erection, barely touching himself through his jeans before he followed Dylan over. When he finished, he pulled off and leaned his head against Dylan's hip. "That was some fucking kiss."

"Mmm, I've always wanted to try that, glad you liked it." Bo leaned back and winked. "Now, Wilma, where's my brontosteak? I need sustenance if there's going to be more of that later when the Rubbles come over for our orgy." He licked a path up Dylan's body until he found his mouth. This time he really did kiss him, hot and hard. Food could wait. This couldn't. Not when there was so little precious time left before Dylan went away. "On second thought, I'm not sharing you with anyone else. Orgy is called off."

"Sounds good to me." Dylan wound his hands in Bo's hair and held him captive. "Sounds so damned good. I'll have second helpings of that." Somehow Bo didn't think the second helping request had anything to do with food.

"How about thirds?" He pressed Dylan to the refrigerator and started working on putting that request on the menu.

"Sounds..." But Dylan never finished that thought. "Fuck."

Chapter Five

"This has to have been the shortest week on record." Bo's voice sliced through the dark. Dylan could hear the unspoken words. He found Bo's hand and linked their fingers. After a week of parades and parties and other post season things that Bo couldn't get out of, the little time they had left was winding down to hours. There were three left, but he didn't tell Bo that. He didn't tell Bo so many things. Like his next assignment. And how much this one scared him. Because he was a Marine, he wasn't supposed to get scared. He was the monster hunter.

"Too short," he agreed, rolling until he found his lover's mouth in the dark. He slid his arm behind Bo's back and pulled him as close as he could. "Need to make the last hours mean something."

"They've all meant something." Bo threw his leg over Dylan's hip and pressed his cock into Dylan's belly. "Even the hours when we had clothes on. I showed you off. People envied me. How is that not something?" Dylan knew the ego was put-on from their early morning post-fuck conversations. The fame scared him. The people who wanted more than he was willing to give them. He couldn't get laid. Not anymore. Too many people knew his face, he couldn't risk it and keep his homosexuality a secret. Women threw themselves at him. Old men wanted to relive their glory days through him. He hated making commercials. He hated whoring himself out just to play a little football.

"Well, it's not easy being the sexy Marine. So many people to fuck. So little time." He pushed Bo's shoulder, shoving him onto his back so that he could crawl up his long body one more time. "Do you know how many phone numbers I threw away from that one party alone?"

"How many of them were men?" That was a sticking point with Bo, that men would give him their numbers. Seems even some of the upstanding pillars weren't averse to having a Marine in uniform give it to them up the ass. Oorah.

"You don't want to know." He started with Bo's nipples, nipping and licking until Bo bucked into him. Their cocks rubbed together as he moved up to Bo's neck. He found his pulse and sucked that patch of skin into his mouth. This time he was going to leave him marked. Biting until he tasted a hint of copper. "You're the only ass I can't get enough of. I wanted to tell them all to fuck off, that I'm yours."

"Next time. We'll tell them next time." Bo held his head gently, while Dylan nipped at the area, pulling up more blood patches to match the first one. "Oh, fuck, you feel so damned good. Want inside you so damned bad."

"It's my turn. I want to see your face this time. I want to see you when you come. I want that memory to take back with me. Of you looking well and truly fucked." He reached for the last of the condoms and found the nearly empty bottle of lube. He didn't wait for permission or for encouragement. Condom in place, he slicked himself and pushed himself between Bo's legs. "Open for me, 'Cephus." The nickname fell from his lips for the first time since he'd heard it.

"Bowen. You called me Hurricane Bowen. Those are your names for me, not that damned name. Bowen." Dylan reached for the bedside lamp as Bo spoke. The dim light exposed tears that Bo tried to hide.

"Bowen." He leaned forward, his hands behind Bo's knees, spreading him as he kissed him. "Hurricane Bowen. My Bo." He whispered, biting his tongue as he pushed inside his lover. "You feel so good. I need to remember this. I need to know that you love me. I mean really love me."

Bo threw his head back as Dylan hit his prostate. The sound that came from his mouth was caught between a scream and a moan. Dylan fought back moisture in his own eyes, knowing that this was Bo's gift to him. He slowed his hurry for Bo. He wanted him to remember the pleasure not the pain. Fire burned in his eyes. Fire that Dylan would carry with him for the next eighteen months.

"I do love you. Really love you. Not just the sex. But god, this is…yeah, right there…" Bo squeezed his arms as he arched his body, trying to force Dylan deeper. "Makes me…harder, right there."

Dylan couldn't hold back anymore. He shoved Bo's legs back farther and rocked into him, seating himself to his balls. He muffled Bo's cry with his mouth. "Going to fuck you hard. Going to make you feel this. Feel me. For months. Going to make you scream my name and forget the others. Going to make you mine." He slammed into him. Riding him hard. Sweat dripped from his nose to roll down Bo's face. Pain etched across his lover's features but Bo met Dylan's thrusts. His cries against Dylan's lips for Dylan alone.

"No others. Just you. Fuck, Dylan can't take any more. Need to come now." Bo sunk his fingers into Dylan's arms, sliding his arms around his back to pull him closer. Nails grazed his spine, along the tattoo that bore his name. "Yours. Now and forever. Please. Oh fuck please."

Dylan reached between them and stroked Bo's cock. He gripped it tight in his hand and fucked him to the rhythm he set with his hips. Bo wrapped his legs around his waist and arched into him. His eyes wide open and wild, he came, roaring Dylan's name. Dylan pumped into him, not letting him come down. Bo shuddered and trembled as Dylan squeezed another orgasm from him. This one stronger than the last. Only then did he let himself go. Only then did he call

Bowen's name while Bo stroked his back. Easing him back to reality, Bo held him wrapped in his long arms and legs. Mouth to mouth. Soft kisses and softer words. And Dylan pretended that the drops that landed on Bo's cheek really were sweat.

Later after a shower and more food, Dylan dressed while Bo lay sprawled on his stomach asleep, one arm thrown over the side of the bed that Dylan had vacated. His name written in scrolling intricate script down the center of Bo's back thrilled him. He was with him. He'd always be with him. He tied his boot and pulled his jeans over his knife sheath. His hands shaking. One last look. He couldn't kiss him. He wanted to. He didn't want to walk out of his life. Not now. Not like this. But it wasn't his choice.

When the job was done, he'd call him. It was all he had. Five minutes here and there. Five minutes to live a lifetime with this man. "Love you," he whispered. He kissed his fingers and waved. It was stupid middle school girl behavior, but it was all he had.

The night was cold and clear when he slipped from the house. He could see stars. There were more up there, he knew. Tomorrow night he'd see different stars but these were the ones he'd dream of. And the one he left sleeping inside. The black SUV pulled up on the street and he met it. His luggage disappeared into the back. And that was it. One week and it was all gone as if it never happened. He'd remember as much as he could for as long as he could.

With one last look at the house, he climbed inside, the driver greeting him by his new rank, "Staff Sergeant." And that was all there was now.

"Private," he replied and they were off.

* * * * *

He knew the exact moment when he was alone. He knew it was coming. He could feel it between them all evening. The frantic need in him. The almost desperate way he tried to hold on. Bo reached for the pillow he'd slept on and pulled it to him. Dylan's scent engulfed him, hitting him like a three hundred pound linebacker. His gut twisted. His heart followed. Eighteen months and fifteen days. That's how long they had. Eighteen months and fifteen days. He'd been counting since the practice field that morning. He'd keep counting. It's all he could do. Count down until the day Dylan came home to him, for good.

He shoved his face into Dylan's pillow and howled. So god damned unfair. But now he knew. And he'd wait.

When Dylan came home, he'd love him six ways from Sunday.

Chapter Six

Dylan called in May. Three long months with no contact with anyone. His mission was successful. Ten minutes. That's all the time he had to talk. Just ten minutes. Bo was grateful for those ten minutes. Training camp started in late July and his life went back full tilt. There wasn't time to worry about why he hadn't heard from Dyl in weeks. The pressure to repeat the previous season was tremendous. But in the infinite wisdom of the powers that be in the front office most of the team was traded or let out of their contracts and this wasn't the same team as last year. Everything they'd worked for and built had to be started all over again from the ground up.

Summer workouts in the heat were killer. And New Orleans was Satan's Sauna in the hot months. So fucking hot and humid, he couldn't breathe some days. Somehow he managed to get through it because he knew what Dylan went through every day was worse. He got to go home to an air conditioned house and a hot tub and a soft bed. Dylan didn't get that. So he worked his ass off. Counting down the days. Eighteen months became twelve months. And seven years to the day since the day that Dylan left crawled slowly by. Just one more year. That was all, just one and they would be together.

August came in a hurry, the final week of the pre-season nearly at an end. Next week, this all became real. Still no word from Dylan. But they'd gone longer without contact. He dragged his helmet off and flipped his braid, hoping for just a hint of a breeze to blow on his neck and down under his pads. His lungs ached from the heavy air. The coaches worked their asses hard. And Bo hated every god damned one of them right now. He was sweating Gator Aide, it was that bad. But his job was secure for another year. No new upstarts straight out of college were going to put him on the bench.

People watched the practice that day, media and some family. His never showed up, his dad was back home doing the same thing on the high school level but from the coaching side and his mom wouldn't come alone. They'd come to the first game of the season. He already made the arrangements. Everything right down to the flight and hotel. It was their thing. The first game and the first home game. Despite the money he sent them, his dad still worked. Despite everything he had now and didn't need, he was alone. Too much.

But there they were. Both of his parents waving from the sidelines. Maybe the heat had finally gotten to him and he was mistaking another guy's mom and dad for his. He grabbed a bottle of water from the water boy and started the jog across the field. They were done for the day. Time to deal with the interviews and the photo ops and he'd rather just go hug his family and fuss at them for not telling him they were coming.

That's when he saw her. Slightly taller than his mother. Same type of hair. Except brown. Straight, styled to the side with a little lift on top. She wore a dress in this heat. A black one. He hadn't seen her since that morning seven years ago when she'd walked in on him and Dylan. And screamed and ran out.

Bo faltered a step, his jog coming to a halt. He couldn't see anything but her. He couldn't hear anything but his own blood pounding through his head as it roared past his ears. He dropped his helmet and the water and just stood there staring at her. She wouldn't be here. Unless. Unless.

"No," he said, shaking his head, hoping he really was hallucinating. "No, no, she can't be here."

"Hey, 'Cephus, you okay, man? You look…" Bo didn't know who was shaking his arm, or who was speaking. He just heard the words. He couldn't look around; he couldn't take his eyes off her. Not even when she started across the field.

"She can't be here. She can't," he told the guy shaking his arm. But she was and he didn't need her to say a word. He could see it in her eyes. "No. It's a lie. No." His legs wouldn't hold him up. His knees screamed at the impact. But not as loud as his heart. "No."

There was noise all around them. Her arms were around his shoulders and she looked down at him. Tears tracked down her face.

"Nooo, it's a fucking lie. Noo. No. God dammit, no. You can't be here, it's all lies. You can't." There were hands on him from all around. He shoved them all off. He couldn't stop staring into her eyes.

"Dammit, Bo, get up. Get up and stop acting like this." His father's voice intruded and in that moment he hated him. Hated him for all the bullshit he'd put Bo through. All the years of riding his ass. Of treating Dylan as if he were dirt under his feet.

"You never liked him. You never got it. You never…he was mine. I won't let him be gone. Not now. Not when he promised. One year. He was coming back to me in one year. We were going to be together. He never lied to me. Never. The only person I ever trusted to tell me the truth. He isn't gone. He isn't dead." Bo tried to shrug off the hands that grabbed his arms. He tried to get away but there were too many. Too many hands. All stronger than him. They dragged him off his knees and across the field into the building, away from the cameras that were recording everything. Away from the mother with the tears who never said a word. But not his father. Never his father.

"Was that why?" Bo screamed at him the moment his ass hit a bench. His father just stood there, looking lost and small next to all of those uniforms around him. "Is that why you hated him, because you knew he loved me? Is that why none of the coaches would help him get a scholarship. You didn't want him going with me. Is it?"

"Bowen…" His dad glanced around at the startled faces. Bo dragged his practice jersey over his head, his pads followed. He couldn't breathe. The room moved. The worn out t-shirt he wore to keep his pads from chaffing suffered a few more rips. "This is grief. He was your best friend. We'll get through this. We'll—"

"He was my everything. My best friend. My first love. My only love. We were going to be together. Twelve months. It's all he had left." He screamed the words as if giving voice to the truth would bring him back. It didn't. Nothing would.

Silence filled the room. His father looked as if he'd been slapped. His teammates backed away. More silence followed when he bent over. Those standing beside him could see the tattoo. He heard the comments.

"He has one just like it. With my name. It's all we had to give each other. I have his high school ring. He has my team ring."

"You need to think about your career right now." This from his dad. Anger in his eyes. His son doing exactly what he'd trained him not to do. Showing weakness. Fuck that noise, Bo knew he was falling apart. He just didn't give a fuck.

"Fuck my career. Fuck football. And fuck you. He's gone and that's all you care about. Saving fucking face. I don't want this without him. His path—his path is ended. And mine...he should have been with me. Here. He'd still be alive. He'd still be..." he felt the sharp stab in his arm, the burn of the drug in his veins. The room cleared quickly after that. "I can't walk this path without him. I can't."

He saw his parents leave with one of the coaches. A couple of the team doctors hustled them from the locker room into the bowels of the training facility and Dale Shannon sat down on the bench right in front of him. His eyes curiously blank. His hands cold when he took Bo's hands. And Bo let himself go then. There wasn't anyone else around to see. Fuck 'em all. He didn't need them. Or this job. His body betrayed him and he lay down on the bench, looking for some relief to his own personal hell. The drug they'd stuck him with finally dragged him under. And that's where he hoped to stay. Fuck 'em, six ways from Sunday….just fuck 'em all.

Chapter Seven

Bo sat uncomfortably on the love seat across from the blonde. She wanted an exclusive and he didn't really know who she was. The next Barbara Walters is what his PR person told him. Hell, he didn't even know his PR's name. He didn't care either. Just some guy his dad hired to deal with the mess he'd created.

"One year ago this weekend, the world watched as you and Sergeant Dylan Sunday were reunited."

"I don't want to talk about him. If that's the exclusive you're looking for, you're not going to get it." Bo shifted to move the microphone pack that was pressing into his spine. "Football. The playoffs. The Super Bowl. What I eat for breakfast, how much I bench. Politics… Whatever… but not about him."

"Okay, Bowen, sure. Earlier tonight, you repeated your Super Bowl win from last year. Congratulations. That's a huge accomplishment."

"Especially when most of the football world would prefer that I'd gone quietly away. I guess." He shrugged, thinking about it. "This last season was difficult. We shouldn't be here but we are."

"You said that most of football would prefer that you had gone away? Care to elaborate on that?"

He knew she was fishing. He wasn't inclined to talk about that any more than he was about Dylan. "Not really, no."

"So what can we talk about? Your work with the Wounded Warrior Project? But that would bring us back to the subject you'd rather not discuss. Dylan Sunday."

She stared him down. He stared back. She knew he was here under duress. "I have more money than I know what to do with, and if it helps..." He shrugged again, evading the real question.

"It's more than money. You made this your personal cause. When so many other projects could use your money and your time. Like gay rights. The only out gay football player in the NFL and you ignore that cause altogether. Why is that?"

"It's not easy being the only queer in the locker room. I'd rather not call any more attention to it. Simple math. Make them forget. They can't forget with it in their faces." He felt disloyal to the other guys struggling with their sexuality in this sport but he shook it off. He wouldn't be the poster boy for anything getting better in football.

"You said this year was tough? Tell me what that means." She cocked her head to the side, waiting for him to step into her carefully laid trap. This was a dance. One he'd side-stepped all season. "The silent treatment isn't working, Bo, people want to know you. They want to know what makes you special but you hide and evade. The photos of you and Dylan Sunday last year made international newspapers. The touching reunion of two best friends separated by war. But you were more than that. His death—"

"I said leave him out of it. He didn't ask to be dragged into this. My parents handled that day wrong. If they hadn't brought the news to practice, then the media wouldn't have seen me fall apart. I'd still be just another tight end. And oh, aren't those jokes just hilarious. It's a fucking position. The locker room jokes weren't funny the first million times. My teammates acted like I was...well, let's just say I figured it out. The fear, they were afraid of me even though they knew me; they were afraid that I'd treat them like they treat their women. Like all of a sudden I'm sizing a guy I work with up for sex and objectifying him. I never did that before and I didn't do it after. But that's how it became. I showered at home. Or alone. I had to run faster, jump higher, play better than everyone on the team just to get the same respect I had last year. Scoring four of the five touchdowns last year to win the Super Bowl didn't matter. I became this inferior person because I am gay."

"But you stayed. You made them respect you. You made them pay attention. You could have left; you didn't have to put yourself through any of this just to prove something. Especially after his death."

"I wanted to. That first week. I envy those players who can play through grief. I wanted to go out on that field and kick ass and take names but I couldn't even drag my ass out of bed that first week. I was ready to hang up my cleats. The owners would have taken my resignation and they would have heaved a huge sigh of relief because they didn't want the drama. They had my contract almost in the shredder; okay, that's just me being dramatic but there was conversation. I could just walk away, and they'd pretend nothing happened, have a nice life. No drama. And certainly no negative press for having a fag on the team."

"But you didn't. And the press would have been worse if you had been let go. Did you ever think about it that way?"

"I didn't. I didn't care what the press thought or said; they didn't matter, none of that mattered. I didn't walk away because Janine wouldn't let me. And yeah, it was brought to my attention that I was paving some roads. Roads I didn't want to pave. I don't want to be the first. The role model for all the closet cases. Or the kids. Kids like me that want to play but can't because of their sexuality. I did that because Janine called me every morning and told me to get my ass out of bed and make her son proud to have known me."

"Janine? Dylan's mother?"

"Yeah, I always called her Ms. Sunday. Because that's what she was to me. Dylan's mom. She picked us up from practice. She sat in the rain to watch our games when we were little. She gave up time at work to make sure Dyl and I had football. My dad coached the high school team, and my mom couldn't take the time. Dylan's dad was military until he retired but we were older then." He knew he'd stepped into her trap when the first smile touched his lips. "Those were great days."

She smiled at him now, a real smile not just a TV smile for the cameras. "And Janine called you every morning."

"She did. I think it became our way of dealing with it. She was all alone now. Her husband and son gone. I was it. My dad still isn't speaking to me. My mom just doesn't know what to say. It's been tough. But Janine would call me, she'd tell me to get my ass out of bed because Dylan wouldn't like that I'm lying there feeling sorry for myself. Get up and run. And then run when you want to stop. So I ran. And I went back to work because she told me to. She reminded me that I used to be the one who ran the bullies off Dylan. And that I'm bigger and meaner than anyone. Don't let them bully you. She told me that as if I was ten again. Stand up for yourself because you're better than everyone. Get up."

"She sounds like a great woman. Dylan would be proud of her."

"I'm sure he is. She needs to know that. She kept me going when I didn't want to. We'll get through what the future brings, Janine and me."

She nodded, he could have sworn he saw tears in her eyes. "I understand there's a legend behind the hair?"

He tugged at a strand then realized what he did and flipped his hair behind him. "I always kept my hair really short. My dad gave me one of those ridiculous buzz cuts every summer when I was little. It helped with the heat and it was easy enough just to rub some soap and rinse and it just really never occurred to me that I was not fashionable. Dylan liked his hair longer, he'd wear it in whatever the current boy band style was.

He owned a hair dryer and a straightening iron, for Christ sake. Should have known then, you know?" He grinned, remembering. "It was cute the way he fussed over his hair. I gave him shit for it. When he went into the Marines and they shaved his head. I think we both mourned. I promised him that I'd never get a haircut again in protest. That was seven and a half years ago. I can't cut my hair until he comes home. I made that promise."

"Given the circumstances, I'm sure he wouldn't mind if you—"

"No. Not until Dylan tells me it's all right."

"Even though that may never happen? I think at some point you'll have to cut some of it off."

"Given the circumstances, yeah. It may never happen. And I get it trimmed once every so often so that it's not down to my ass. One day I'll be able to get to a point that I can let go and then I'll donate it to that group that makes wigs for cancer patients."

"Locks of Love?"

"Yeah, them. I'm not there yet. I might never get there. Besides I like having long hair. Promise or not."

"One year ago tonight, I tried to get you to sit down for an interview but you disappeared. I thought you were just ditching me."

"Yeah, sorry. I had something more important to do that night."

"More important than celebrating your win with your team?"

"Yeah. More important than that."

"Would you tell me if I asked nicely?"

He thought about it; he could lie. Or he could look her in the eye and make her wish she'd never asked. "Reuniting with Sergeant Dylan Sunday. We had six years to get out of our system and only a week to do it in."

She turned red; her eyes went wide when she caught on to his meaning. "Oh." The laugh was nervous and a little embarrassed. "Well, I did ask. Guess that's what I get for being nosy."

"Pretty much." It was his turn to go red faced. Now that it was out and he couldn't take it back.

"One last question, Bo, if you don't mind."

"Sure, it's not like you didn't get me to bare my damned soul as it was, may as well go for my throat." He couldn't think where she might go next and she paused long enough that he started to sweat.

"Do you remember those old breaks right after the Super Bowl when some reporter shoves a microphone in front of the quarterback's face and asks him what he's going to do now that he's won the big game?"

"Yeah, I think so. It was usually a Disney commercial moment, right?"

"That would be the one." She paused for effect. "So now that you've won your second Super Bowl, Bowen Murphy, what are you going to do now?"

He knew she was waiting for some dumb answer. Some trite commercial moment. He also knew more than she did. "I'm going to fly to DC in about an hour and I'm going to bring Dylan Sunday home."

* * * * *

He sat unmoving in the chair. Almost as if he wasn't really alive. Bo had to stop in the doorway to catch his breath. He held on to the frame until his knees stopped shaking. Two months ago, they'd received word that Dylan had been found. Alive. But it was bad. Bo had flown Janine to the military hospital in Germany as soon as he'd been transferred. She'd been with him ever since. Calling Bo every morning to keep him up to date. Dylan had yet to speak. He was alive and breathing on his own but that's about as good as it got.

For months after the Killed in Action news came, they'd waited for a body. For months, Janine tried to get information. She just wanted to bring him home. But red tape was tying everything up and she was getting transferred from one department to another until the people she spoke to didn't even know who she was talking about. Finally, in November she got one of Dylan's commanders on the phone. She didn't even know how it happened. And the news was horrifying. Dylan wasn't killed. But he was missing. He'd been part of a protection detail for some CIA agent and they'd been attacked. Dylan, the agent, and another Marine had survived, but were missing. And no one thought to make sure the family had correct data. The commander apologized. Profusely. And in December, they'd stumbled upon him and one of the other prisoners while on patrol. That same commander called Janine personally.

He'd been starved and tortured for five months. And this was what was left of the man Bo loved. This husk. This unmoving shell. Dead eyes staring out the window. He blinked every few seconds but that's all he did.

Janine sat in a chair by his bed. She looked almost as haggard as her son. Almost. She laid her e-reader on the bedside table and came to wrap her arms around his neck. "So proud of you. And so happy you're here."

That's more than he got from his parents that morning. Of course, he would have had to have taken his dad's call to know why he'd contacted him. Proud that he won another Super Bowl. Proud that he'd scored five touchdowns instead of four from the previous year. Proud that he didn't break down on national television. What the fuck ever.

"How is he?" He couldn't take his eyes off the man in the wheelchair. He had hair now. It was a mess, unruly, looking more like someone had taken a set of rusty sheers to his head than anything else. But it was hair.

"The same. Today's a good day. He slept last night. Or at least he didn't scream." She patted his cheek, there were tears in her eyes. And Bo knew that she thought Dylan was better off dead. She'd told him as much in the early days. Before he began to heal. Before he could sit up on his own. Just before. "I'm going to go get some breakfast. And walk around. I'll be back in an hour." She stopped just outside the door. "I watched you on TV last night. It was a good interview. He would be proud of you. I'm sure he's proud of you."

Bo just nodded. He didn't know what to say. Or if the words would come out without tears. So many times he'd cried on her shoulder. She held him up. When he should have been the one holding her up. She nodded back and walked past the nurse's station, calling the nurses by name as she passed.

He stood for another moment before going inside. This was Dylan. Broken Dylan but still Dylan and he would do everything he could, spend every penny he had and beg borrow or steal what he didn't have to fix him. He dropped to his knees beside the chair.

The hand on the armrest seemed skeletal. Bo touched him anyway. Taking the hand and linking their fingers. He was so cold. "I'm sorry it took so long to get here. I wanted to come as soon as I knew. I couldn't get away. Your mom, man, she just took over, and she kept me from walking away from it all. Even when you were found. She made me finish the job. I wanted to be here. I wanted to be with you."

A blink answered him. Blue eyes stared at the cold winter sky outside the window. He didn't squeeze Bo's hand. "One year ago this week, we were together. Do you remember? Seems so long ago. Like decades really. But it was just a year. I love you so damned much, Dyl. I'm going to do everything I can to fix this. All of my money. All of it. I'll give it all up. Football. Everything to make you well again."

He reached into his pocket and pulled out the ring. Gold with black and white diamonds in a fleur de lis pattern and a bunch of roman numerals sparkled in the light. "This one is from last year. I won another one last night. That one is yours. It was for you. But for right now I want you to have this one." He slipped the ring on Dylan's hand noticing how loose the ring fit him. "And as soon as the doctors say we can, I'm going to take you home. To Florida, if that's where you want to go. Or to New Orleans. Wherever you want to be."

He couldn't take the stillness. He couldn't look into the perfect face of his love and not see any recognition at all. He laid his head on Dylan's lap. Just for a moment. Trying to keep the tears from coming. He pretended not to see the one empty footrest on the wheelchair. He just needed a minute. He stopped breathing when shaking fingers wound through his hair. He didn't dare move.

"Don't cut it. I won't give you permission. Not even for charity." The words were shaky and not much above a whisper. When Bo glanced up, he saw tears streaming down his lover's face.

He took the hand from his hair and held it tight. "I won't. I swore I wouldn't. I promised. Not until you come home for good."

He caught Dylan when he pitched forward. His body so thin beneath the heavy robe. Two thin arms wrapped around him, skeletal fingers digging into his back. "I want to go home. So much. I don't remember home."

The words were choked with tears and his body shook as he sobbed. "I'll remind you. I'll tell you stories that will make your hair curl. Okay, curl more than it is now."

Bo saw the nurse in the doorway. He shook his head when she started for them. She stopped, her hand going to her mouth but she didn't leave. "Sounds so good. You sound so good."

Bo didn't care if it was against hospital rules. He didn't care who saw. He reached beneath Dylan's legs and pulled him out of the chair. One foot bumped against his thigh as he turned to sit on the bed. Dylan no more than a lapful now. He held him as close and as tight as he dared for fear of breaking him. "You're alive. That's all that matters. We can fix all the rest. We will fix all the rest. Love you so damned much."

Dylan cried harder. His arms like iron bands around Bo's shoulders. "I'm not breakable. You won't hurt me. Just take me home."

Bo saw another figure enter the room in his peripheral. He turned his head slightly to see Janine standing there. Her eyes round and glassy. The nurse cried silent tears, her hand over her mouth. Janine did the same. The line so fine. They all knew it. Even Bo knew this could be temporary. Only time would tell if Dylan stayed with them. Or if he would return to the hell that trapped him inside his mind.

"Yeah, Sunday, we're going to go home." He pressed a kiss to Dylan's forehead. "Maybe get married and adopt a couple of kids, or dogs. I'm probably better with dogs. We're going to do it right this time. Walk the same path for a while." He didn't flinch from the words. Dylan was missing a leg. He wasn't paralyzed. This could be fixed. "We will walk the path together, right?"

Dylan sat up, his eyes clear, his hands still shook, but he seemed more like himself. His voice stronger when he spoke this time. "Hurricane Bowen. Yeah, I can do that. You might have to carry me for a while."

"No, man, that's not how this works. You're going to carry yourself.

You're going to get your ass up and brush off the grass and the chalk and you're going carry your ass across that goal line. You got me across it enough times. This time, I'm going to be the one pushing you. We're just going to walk this one off, and play through the pain. Okay? Just me and you. Okay, just me and you."

But Dylan didn't answer. His eyes were closed. He breathed. He was alive. A smile played across his lips. Bo held him tight, finally letting go all of the fear and pain he'd carried since August. He cried it all out. Sitting there holding his lover while he slept. Dylan Sunday, the larger than life force of nature that thought he was a hurricane. Bo knew the truth. Dylan Sunday was the calm, his center, the eye of his storm and he could no more live without him than he could live without breathing. And now it was his turn to be that for Dylan. His center. They'd get through this. Just like they always had. Together. Because that's the only path left. The one they'd walk together.

Epilogue

July

Two years later

"What do you mean I've got to beat a gimp to win a spot? What kind of fucked up test is that?"

The new receivers were entitled little assholes. Bo heard everything, his hackles up, ready to knock heads. The new QB put his hand on Bo's shoulder and shook his head. They had work to do learning the new playbook. Then he laughed because the look on Dylan's face at the comment was priceless. The kid didn't know what Dylan Sunday could do with just one leg.

"That gimp is a US Marine who lost his leg so your sorry ass could have this chance to be on one of the best teams in the NFL." Dale Shannon shouted over the chatter. "And you will say 'yes, Sir' when he tells you to run. When he tells you to run or to jump you say 'Sir Yes Sir.' And you better outrun him and out-jump him. Or you will not have a position on this team. You will be cut and sent home crying to your mama."

Dylan took off and the rest of the pack was left in the dust. He looked good. Healthy. Shannon bringing him in as an assistant coach was probably the one thing that pushed him back into the world.

"It's a pity they won't let him try out. He'd make one hell of a quarterback," the new kid said as they watched Dylan come in a close third out of ten.

"That's your job you're giving away if the commissioner ever let him have a chance." Bo reminded him.

"Yeah, well, I might have been born at night but it wasn't last night. I know talent when I see it. And he's got it," the rookie said almost in awe.

"He walked a different path. He has no regrets." Dylan caught his eye and winked. Bo felt his face grow hot. "Besides he's a masochist. He likes inflicting pain. He'd have been a drill sergeant if he'd stayed in. I'm sure of it."

*****

Dylan watched Bo flush with anger from across the field. He could feel his eyes on him all afternoon. At first the attention bothered him, but as the day wore on he realized it was comforting. Having Bo ready to take on his whole team for him, well, it made Dylan feel all warm and fuzzy inside.

He'd lost that ability to feel anything for a long time. Bo made him feel. Bo made him live. And he got up every morning put the damned blade on and he ran; well, first he walked. He walked the path around the property that they made together several times a day. When he could run without pain, he ran. And his mind started to work again. Loving Bo again took time. Letting him touch him sometimes was the hardest, and Bo gave him the space he needed. He knew that every time he rejected him that Bo hurt. But he gave him time. Nearly a year. God, it was a horrible year. Everything went wrong in that year. The team went to hell. Bo's dad died of a heart attack while they were still estranged. Just…that was what did it for him. Being there for Bo after that. Letting Bo touch him without flinching.

This was a piece of cake. Making a bunch of spoiled college brats coming in with egos bigger than the Super Dome eat dust. Yeah, this was easy. He could do this all day long. As long as he got to go home with the star of the team when it was all said and done.

And Bo was the star. The quarterback whose arm gave out last season and cost them the season was gone. As was most of the team. Management let the gay business rest after his second Super Bowl win. Gay or not, the man sold tickets and won games. And that was the hard line decision. Money over politics. Money always won when it came down to it.

These kids made comments because they were stupid. Comments that were shut down real fast. "I was special forces. I lost my leg because a bunch of assholes thought it would be funny to torture me and kill my friends. I lived and they didn't," Dylan said softly. "My name is Dylan Sunday, if you didn't know, and I have a reputation to uphold. Cross me and I'll fuck you up six ways from Sunday."

After that, Dylan didn't hear a peep. He smiled as his lover flew across the field, his hair whipping behind him as he jumped to catch the impossible throw from the new quarterback. Hurricane Bowen was on the loose and Dylan's heart flew with him with every step he took. Oh yeah, this year was going to be a great year. He could feel it in his bones. They were together now and the world had no idea what the two of them were capable of. But they were going to find out. Every Sunday from now until the day Bowen decided he was ready to walk another path. And Dylan would be right there by his side.

The End

About the Author:

Born and raised in the wilds of north west Florida, I currently make my home in Mobile, Alabama where I attended the University of South Alabama. My interests are as diverse as the topics about which I write. I love to quilt, cook, and troll resale stores for bargains. Being a good southern girl I love football and fried food. I write southern themed spicy romance of the het and gay variety. Because love doesn't care who you are.

Mercy's Website:
http://mercyceleste.blogspot.com/

Other books by Mercy:

@ Liquid Silver Books

Double Coverage
Wicked Game
Let it Go

@ Total E Bound Books

Behind Iron Lace

And coming in October:
Under a Crescent Moon

The indies @ MJC Press

In From the Cold
The 51st Thursday
Midnight Clear
Beyond Complicated
Six Ways from Sunday